AT THE BOTTOM OF THE STAIRS

Chloe Banks lives on the edge of Dartmoor with her husband and two young sons. Her novel, *The Art of Letting Go*, was published by Thistle Publishing (2014) and was shortlisted for the People's Book Prize. Since then she has concentrated on short and flash fiction, gathering a handful of publications, listings and prizes along the way. A scientist by education, she now focuses on scriptwriting, with a little bit of flash fiction here and there. When not taming words or children, she can usually be found wandering the moor or eating chocolate. Or both.

ALSO BY CHLOE BANKS

The Art of Letting Go

At the Bottom of the Stairs

Chloe Banks

REFLEX PRESS

First published in 2022 by Reflex Press
Abingdon, Oxfordshire, OX14 3SY
www.reflex.press

A CIP catalogue record of this book is
available from the British Library.

ISBN: 978-1-914114-09-0

1 3 5 7 9 10 8 6 4 2

Printed and bound in Great Britain by
Imprint Digital, Upton Pyne, Exeter.

Cover design: Paul Banks
Cover images: Smilyk Pavel, Olivier
Le Moal, Rio T / Shutterstock.com

www.reflex.press/at-the-bottom-of-the-stairs/

To Digory and Wilfred, and for all children (young and old) who climb trees and dream of flying

To my dearest Emma,
with so much love,

Anne x

2022

CONTENTS

Everything After Now

Tomorrow they will laugh about this. In the hotel restaurant, while Tommy piles his plate with bacon, and Rachel spoons fruit compote onto her yoghurt, they will glance sideways at each other. They'll laugh at how two glasses of house white could have made them forget fifty-two years, two happy marriages. *It was nothing*, they'll say. *A moment of madness.* And Rachel will take a table by the window, and Tommy will take a table by the door.

On Sunday night, Tommy will lie next to Anabelle in their super-king-sized bed, wide-eyed in the dark. She will turn to him and say, *How was the exhibition? Did you sell any pictures? What was the hotel like?* And he will say, *Fine. Two. Full of retired tourists.* When Anabelle wants to know why he is so quiet, he'll tell her that he met a friend from long ago who made him realise how old he is. She will laugh and reach for his hand beneath the covers.

Sometime next month, Rachel will be baking Spider-Man cupcakes with her granddaughter. As she presses the rice paper shapes from their sheet and passes them into buttercreamed fingers, she will find herself wondering if, in another life, Olivia might have had Tommy's cowlick instead of Francis's curls. That evening, as Francis snorts over *The News*

Quiz while they peel potatoes together at the sink, that other life will haunt her. The life where she took Tommy's ring instead of her mother's advice will hover at the edges of her vision, dissolving as she turns to look.

In October, Tommy will catch sight of Rachel again across the foyer of the National. She will be laughing with a man who can only be her son. The sight will bring Tommy to a standstill, breathless, until Anabelle touches his arm, draws him towards the usher selling programmes. Tommy and Rachel will spend three hours sitting three rows apart, and Rachel won't see him until they are about to step into adjacent taxis. Her hand will touch her lips in shock and, although he'll know it was involuntary, he will catch the kiss anyway and hold it hot in his memory.

Nine months from now, Rachel will see an obituary in *The Times*: *Renowned artist. Devoted husband.* It will say nothing about his childhood sweetheart; no mention of his second-hand mohair jacket or the way he whistled *The Entertainer* as he waited at the end of Station Road, a bunch of daffs in his hand. *Private funeral for close family only.*

But now there is none of that. In the hotel bar, with Francis at the vintage car rally and Anabelle eighty miles away, there is no future, no past. Five decades slip away in one chance reunion. Rachel is seventeen again, and her parents have not yet cajoled her into setting aside a man who draws in pen and ink and who has no money and no prospects of making any. Tommy hasn't yet failed to convince them of his worth. Age and expectations have not painted their words with caution.

I'm happily married, but...
I love my husband, but...
It's always been you.
I still miss you.

For one afternoon – one drink in the bar, one walk on the terrace – they can be the dreamers they once were. *Let's run away together.* And everything before now has disappeared. And nothing after now matters.

Laika, 1957

The day Rachel falls out of the walnut tree is the day they send that dog into space. Two things higher than nature intended, Katherine thinks to herself later. She doesn't think this at the time. When she sees her daughter falling from the bare branches of the tree, she doesn't have time to think. In the half minute it takes her to run from the kitchen window to the back door and across the garden, the single thought pounding in time to her heart and her feet is *no no no no no*.

Rachel is motionless when Katherine drops to the ground at her side. Is she breathing? Does she have a pulse? How do you check for a pulse?

She is still fumbling with Rachel's wrist when Rachel opens her eyes. 'Mamma?'

Katherine resists the urge to smack her, to kiss her, to shake her, to cry.

Rachel looks up into the branches and frowns. 'Did I fall?'

'Yes.' Katherine closes her eyes. 'A long way. You were too high again. What did I tell you about going too high? It's nearly dark out here.'

'I was trying to see her, Mamma.'

'Trying to see who?'

'The dog. The one on the wireless. The one they put in a rocket.' Rachel sits up. 'I thought if I climbed high enough, I might see a light or something – it might be her spaceship.'

'You're a daft thing,' Katherine says. 'I don't know how you got to be so daft.' This isn't true. She has a good idea how Rachel got to be how Rachel is, but she tries not to think about it.

She holds up her hand. 'Here – how many fingers can you see?'

She might not know how to find a pulse, but Katherine knows all about concussion. She had it herself as a child. Not from climbing trees – she has never climbed a tree in her life – but from a cyclist bowling her down outside the butcher's. Katherine knows about double vision and vomiting and con-fusion, so even though Rachel skips ahead of her back into the house, she finds herself unable to stop watching. All the time she is finishing the interrupted washing-up and making eggs on toast for their tea, she watches her daughter at the kitchen table, drawing a picture of a dog in a spaceship on the back of the gas bill.

When Rachel was a baby, Katherine spent hours watching her: the flicker of her closed eyelids, the rise and fall of her chest, the silent suckling movements her mouth made in her sleep. She watched her when she was a toddler crouched in the flowerbeds conversing with beetles, watched her as she lined up her teddies for secret missions. When had that stopped? When had watching her become nothing more than watching out for her: holding her hand when they crossed Markham Road, feeling her forehead when her eyes were too bright, telling her to get down when she climbed too high?

As Katherine watches, she thinks two things. Firstly, they should never have sent that poor creature into space like that.

Secondly, there is a wild horse in her daughter that she knows she must tame, and she's terribly afraid that she doesn't know how. Katherine has never been wild. She has only deviated from The Safe and The Tame once. That was enough. Too much. Any wildness in Rachel she gets from her father. Rachel has Katherine's hair and flat feet; she has her father's inability to keep still, his need to climb to the top of a walnut tree to see into space.

When Peter gets home that night, Katherine asks him to check on Rachel.

'Check she's asleep, not unconscious.'

Peter doesn't know how he is going to tell the difference, but he goes anyway.

Rachel is not in bed. She's sitting on her windowsill, curtains wide, nightie pulled over her knees.

'Do you think she's OK, Daddy?' She holds out her hand to draw him closer. 'That dog. Do you think she likes it up there?'

'Well...' Peter thinks about this. He has never lied to Rachel about anything other than the things he must always lie about. 'I think maybe she's a bit scared.'

'It's a big adventure, though, isn't it?'

'It is.' He strokes Rachel's hair. 'And it will teach all those clever space scientists lots of things.' He points at the gibbous moon hanging above the walnut tree. 'One day, a man may even walk up there because of what they learn from that dog.'

'Or a girl?' Rachel leans her head against his shoulder. 'A girl like me?'

Peter sighs. 'It wouldn't surprise me if a girl just like you ended up on the moon one day.'

They wait in silence together, watching the sky for a sign that a stray mongrel is circling above them. Peter is just about to send Rachel back to bed when his daughter lifts her hand to the glass.

'She's not coming back, is she?' she says. 'They won't be able to get her down.'

Peter wishes he didn't know the answer. He wishes he could tweak at the edges of the story, pulling it straight until the dog up there finds a path back to earth – lands in a shower of ticker tape. He wishes all endings involved safe landings.

'No,' he says. 'I don't suppose they will.'

He lifts Rachel from the windowsill and carries her to bed as he did when she was three and they had to say goodbye to the garden every evening.

'Goodnight, *mon petit chat.*'

'Daddy?'

Peter stops in the doorway, captured – enraptured – by those two syllables.

'If you're sometimes a bit scared, and if you can't go back, is it still an adventure?'

Peter looks at her in the finger of moonlight, bony and bright on her blanket. And not for the first time, not for the last, he doesn't know what to say.

Head in the Clouds

She will be a giant soon. Up she goes: up past the top of the porch, beyond the tangles of the rambling rose; up past her bedroom window and the copy of *Bunty* lying open on her bed; up past the eaves, over the chimney pots.

She is growing faster now, shooting towards the grinning moon, pale in the blue morning sky. When she laughs, her breath catches the feathers of the crow in the top of the red oak, stirring him from sleep. From up here, she can see the newsagent on the corner and empty school playground on Humbleby Street. If she's careful not to go giddy, she can look down at the black Mary Janes she's wearing-in for next term and, beside them – far, far below – Mamma hanging out bed sheets like discarded angel wings, bright white from the wash.

When she reaches the clouds, she breathes in a lungful of soft: Daddy's scarf, Mamma's hair, the patch on Mr Ted where she still strokes him to sleep even though she is too old for all that. As they shift and break up around her, she can see mountains with no tops and tigers in jungle shadows. She can see the Eiffel Tower and the Statue of Liberty and people eating ice cream of three different flavours at once.

She can see all the way to the end of the world.

And when Mamma's voice climbs its way up through the lazy, summer air – *are you fetching those pegs, or not?* – and she begins to shrink back down into herself again, she wonders if, when the crow wakes, it's because he dreams of falling.

Dead Cert

'I've sorted it,' he says, and his hands close round your arm. 'Your mam's going to be OK, Tommy. I promise.'

This version of Dad always makes you uneasy. This is Grand National Dad, FA Cup Final Dad, the Dad who fingers the slip in his pocket as Sugar Ray Robinson takes to the ring. This frantic mania of hope is not new, but there is a sharper edge to it today. There's a kind of joy in his words, a madness – a panic that spills out of him across the kitchen, settling on the unwashed breakfast bowls, the crumbs where you hacked up the heel of Tuesday's loaf to take to school for lunch.

'I went to the church on the way back from hospital,' he says. 'Not that little chapel place your mam likes, but the proper church – the big one behind Stanley Rec.' He releases your arm, only to take hold of your shoulders, faces level. 'I got down on my knees, Tommy. Don't ever think your dad's too proud to beg. Not for your mam – I'm never too proud to beg for your mam. And I made a deal with God. I'm going to clean up, Tommy. No more beer. No more horses or the pools. None of it. I'm going to go dead straight from now on, and God's going to make your mam get better. That's our deal, you understand?'

Not really. First Dad told you Mam's cough was nothing, then it was just a little something, and then suddenly it was Everything. It was coming home to an empty house and beans on toast for tea three days straight and not knowing how to get the grass stains off your school shirt. And now he is telling you that the cough will be nothing again. He will make it nothing by coming straight home from the garage, by turning the bookie's runners away from the door. You don't understand how that works.

'I know I've not always been the best dad to you.' He has not yet let go of you. This is the longest you can remember him ever touching you. 'But I've never hurt you, have I?'

You shake your head. No, he's never hurt you.

'Some men who like their drink hit their wives and little ones, you know that?'

You nod. Yes, you know that.

'But I've never done that. I'd never do that. I love you and your mam, and I'm going to make sure she's OK. I'm going to be a good dad to you now, right? We're going to go to the rec after school tomorrow. We'll play football. When your mam's well again, we'll save up and take the train to the seaside.' His voice rises like an Epson Derby commentator in the final furlong. 'We'll get ice cream.'

In the last rays of afternoon sun, his face lights with a memory, and he drops your shoulders, reaches into his tool bag. 'Look, I got us these.' He pulls out two tins: evaporated milk, peaches. 'We can have a little celebration, Tommy. You and me. We'll celebrate that your mam's going to get well again. Those doctors don't know about my deal with God – but I'll tell them tomorrow, and they'll change their minds then, you see if they don't.'

He scrabbles in the drawer for the tin-opener, crashes two bowls onto the table.

'I'm going to get us some money.' The peaches slop into the bowls, juice splattering on the grimy tabletop. 'When your mam comes back, she'll need good food and won't be able to take in any ironing for a bit. So I'm going to find something to sell.' His eyes skip across the room, searching for inspiration. 'Or I'll borrow something. Jim at the garage knows a bloke who lends money to people like us – no questions asked.'

You watch as the milk streams from the can into your bowl, and you wish he wasn't talking so fast. You wish the words that fire from his mouth feel like the truth when they hit you. You want him to use a different voice – not the one he used when Nan gave you that shilling for your birthday, and he told you Pearly Prince was a dead cert, or the one he used when he told Mam that Arsenal would win the cup for sure.

'Money,' he says. 'Money's the thing. Make sure you've always got money, Tommy, right? Whatever else you do with your life, remember money's the thing.'

He throws a spoon to you, laughs uproariously when you fumble it to the floor. 'When you've had that, you could draw your mam a picture, couldn't you? Dead proud of your pictures she is – always showing them to everybody. Draw her some bluebells – she'll love that.'

Bluebells are wrong. You don't want to draw bluebells. Bluebells are what Mam puts on her dad's grave for his birthday, even though somebody always stamps on them. It's not enough – even after forty years – for his name to be missing from the War Memorial, they have to stamp on his memory, on Mam's grief. Bluebells mean dead people and shame and *shot at dawn*. They're not what you draw for somebody who's going to get better.

'Tommy?' He is watching you, spoon hovering above his bowl, a drop of milk hanging from the end. 'It'll be alright, I promise. Your mam's a fighter. And we've God on our side now too. We're on to a winner there, no mistake.'

He puts down his spoon, reaches over the table to take your hand. And you search his face for something new, something different from all the other times.

'I've got it sorted now.' He grins that wide, certain grin. 'We can't possibly lose.'

Education

Rachel and Maggie are halfway over the wall when Mrs Marsh catches them. And even though they tell her that they'll be five minutes late for school if they go round, she says climbing the wall is unladylike and stands at the front gate until they're out of sight round the corner of the road.

They run the last two streets to school and get there just as the bell goes. Even though they slow to a walk when they reach the gate, Mr Brisket across the road tells on them, and they have to stay in at break anyway. For *unbecoming behaviour* Mrs Croft says, but it's not fair because they kept their berets on the whole way and held down their skirts so they didn't flap.

That evening, Rachel asks Mamma what it's like to be a lady and whether it matters very much. Mamma says it's hard work sometimes, but if you behave like a lady, then people will treat you like a lady, and if you don't, they won't, and that's what matters. When Dad gets home, Rachel asks him if she has to be a lady yet, and he says no, not yet, not quite yet. And she tells Maggie what he said the next morning when she calls for her, but they go the long way round anyway.

Valentina, 1963

The newspaper cutting is half-tucked under Rachel's pillow. She catches sight of it as she perches on the edge of the bed to peel off her itchy school tights. Dad must've put it there when he came home for lunch. He must've snipped it out before adding his morning paper to the shoe-shining, window-cleaning stack in the garage. She can imagine him folding the paper back on itself so that Mamma wouldn't notice the missing page and want to know what nonsense he'd been putting into her head.

The woman in the picture is not dressed in a spacesuit. She's in a plain white T-shirt, her eyes fixed on something to the left of shot. She's not smiling. She looks fierce – not angry, just fierce. She looks ready.

Rachel crosses to the Dansette on her desk. She slides the *Blue Hawaii* soundtrack from its sleeve as if Elvis might shield her – as if his voice might prevent her thoughts reaching Mamma's ears in the kitchen. Rachel is meant to be thinking about *Wuthering Heights*. She's meant to be writing three to four pages in her best cursive on the subject of Emily Brontë's use of weather. She isn't meant to be reading newspaper clippings about a woman beyond the edge of the world.

Once her homework is spread on the desk, Rachel returns to the bed. She looks at the woman again, runs the words around her tongue. *Tereshkova. Vostok. Chaika.* They are wild words, strange words, words that light something inside her. Her gaze goes to the window and the cloud-heavy sky beyond. The woman is still up there, the newspaper says. Somewhere. She is circling the world, seventeen thousand miles an hour, sun rising and setting on her every ninety minutes. She is as high as it is possible to be.

Rachel lies back on her pillow, clutching the cutting to her chest. Eyes closed, she launches herself up through the ceiling of her bedroom, up beyond the housetops, shattered plaster and tiles streaming from her. She soars higher until England spreads below her – the rolling hills of the poems she learns at school. In another second, she can see the dust-yellow of the Sahara, then the North Pole, the curve of the horizon, the darkness beyond. She hovers there, tucked tight in her capsule.

A wave of cramp brings Rachel back to Earth. She rolls onto her side. Do cosmonauts have periods, she wonders. Up there, looking down on a planet not made for women, might that woman's body – fierce and ready – be in sync with her own? But no. They must have drugs for that. Or, at least, they would've timed the flight to fit. Even the first woman in space cannot be allowed to be so treacherously female.

Mamma's footsteps on the stairs send Rachel to her desk. She slides the newspaper cutting under her French exercise book. By the time the door opens, Rachel's head is bent over an examination of Lockwood's appearance in a blizzard.

'Do you have a lot of homework tonight?' Mamma places the pile of ironed school blouses on Rachel's bed.

'A bit.' Rachel waves a hand at the scattering of books: English essay, trigonometry, a handful of French verbs to conjugate.

'I'll leave you to it then.' Mamma leans down to kiss Rachel's head as she passes. 'You're a good girl, Rachel.' She turns the volume knob on the Dansette down a quarter turn. 'Dinner at six.'

Rachel's cosmonaut stays hidden as she works. Even after dinner, when she can hear Frankie Laine crooning from the gramophone below, the clink and glug of sherry being poured into two glasses – even then, when she is safe from accusations of daydreaming and time-wasting – Rachel leaves the clipping out of sight. She feels unsettled and hopeful and full of a strange, jealous joy. She tries to feel fierce.

When it's time for bed, she leaves the curtains wide, the midsummer dusk fading into night. She slides her cosmonaut beneath the mattress – lies on the crumpled sheet, feeling the heat of stardust rising from between the springs below. And just before sleep pulls her into space, she looks once more at the window and presses her hands to her cramping belly.

Of Course You Won't

You won't fall for her, of course. You don't have time for girls. Certainly not girls like this one: girls who appear halfway down Gargrave Street, barefoot in the branches of a tree, singing 'Hippy Hippy Shake'.

She is the sort of girl your dad warned you about. Not your mum – Mum warned you about girls in short skirts and red lipstick, ones who already had boyfriends or who kissed you on a first date. Dad knew better. He warned you about the unexpected girls – the girls you couldn't take your eyes off and didn't know why. He warned you about girls who pull you in the second you look at them. *Them's the troubling ones*, he said. *Them's the ones you'll end up marrying if you're not careful.*

'Are you looking at my knickers?' She scowls down at you from her tree branch.

You take a step away. 'Course not. Just saw you up there and wondered if you needed help getting down.'

She jumps, landing at your feet. 'Nope.'

'Right,' you say, lowering your voice a tone. 'I'll be getting along then.'

That's your cue to move. You should walk on. You're not doing girls anymore, remember?

You stoop to pick up the pencil tin spilling from her satchel. 'What were you doing up there?'

'Climbing.' She takes the tin from your hand. 'Climbing a. ' waiting for my bus. It's always late.'

You watch as she re-ties her shoes, re-plaits her hair, re-places her beret. She stuffs the tin back into her satchel and looks at you. 'What were you doing down here while I was up there?'

'Passing,' you say, and then – because you forget for a moment your promise to your mum that you'll concentrate on your drawing, and your promise to your dad that you'll concentrate on getting rich, and your promise to yourself that you will avoid girls who will stop you doing either of those things – you say, 'I was on my way home. Just been out sketching, actually.'

'Sketching what?'

'People mostly.' Deep breath. 'I'm an artist.'

You've practised these three words so many times, and yet you don't sound casual and suave. They lack the gravity, the coolness you intended, even when you belatedly brush a speck from your turtleneck, stick one hand in the pocket of your plaid chinos. You wish you had a cigarette to draw on.

She laughs. 'What's your real job? Or are you still at school?'

Surely she can see that you're no schoolboy? It has been almost a year since you last wore your tie and blazer. You must be a year older than her – more probably. You're a man now. On your own in the world. She must be able to tell.

'How do you know being an artist isn't my real job?'

She wrinkles her nose. 'Is it?'

For a second, you think of lying. But if you lie, you would have to remember to lie again next time. Not that there'll be a next time, of course. 'I work in the stock room at White's.'

'You're a shop boy!' She laughs again but stops when she sees your face. 'I'm allowed to laugh – I'm a shop girl. I do the confectionary counter in Austin Cook's on Saturdays.' She shrugs. 'It's money, isn't it? For the pictures or something. It's not forever.'

Austin Cook's is on the High Street, four doors away from White's. It would only take two minutes of a lunch hour to walk over there. Only five to say hello. Not that you will, of course. You won't do that. Just as you won't find yourself walking down this street again at the same time tomorrow and the day after. Definitely not the day after that. Not for a girl who sings pop songs at the top of her voice and jumps out of trees and talks about her knickers.

You glance at your watch and wonder what time she takes lunch on a Saturday.

With a hiss, a bus appears round the corner. The girl steps forward, raises her hand to the conductor. She slings her satchel over her shoulder.

'Nice meeting you,' she says without looking at you. 'Good luck with the drawings.'

The bus clunks to a stop by a sign a dozen yards off. She hurries towards it, and you turn away. The smooth bark of the tree – the way the colours run into each other and out again – catches your eye. You lay a hand on the bottom branch. When was the last time you climbed a tree?

'Be careful.' She is standing on the open rear platform, watching you. 'Shouldn't like you to get hurt.'

You have a primal urge to do it – to show this girl how fast you can climb, how high you can go. But the bus is already at the turn of the road, and you take your hands from the branch. It's not worth the risk. One slip, and you'd end up falling after all.

Staircase Wit

'We should have a phrase for it,' he says, kicking at the dirt beneath the swing. 'The French have one.'

Rachel slides into the other swing, pulling the hem of her skirt down towards her knees. Tommy has not stopped talking all the way from the offie. She likes that about him. She's never met a boy who talks like him – talks about small things as if they are big, big things as though they are within reach. She grabs the chains and tips her head back to look at the clouds lazing their way past the tops of the ash trees. She feels as if she is floating – caught in a current of warm air between the park and the sky.

'They call it *l'esprit de l'escalier*,' Tommy says. 'Staircase wit. It's that thing where you think of a smart answer when it's too late – when you're at the bottom of the stairs and there's no going back up to say all the things you should have said.'

He has been telling her all the things he should've said all the way down Coronation Road. By the time they'd pushed their way through the kissing gate into the deserted park on the edge of Stanley Rec, Tommy had thought of half a dozen ways he could've persuaded the man behind the counter to sell them his cheapest bottle of white after all.

Rachel is glad they have no more wine. Before today she has never had more than the two fingers in the bottom of a tumbler Dad offers her over the roast every Sunday. The half-bottle she has already shared with Tommy is making her light-headed. It isn't unpleasant, but she doesn't want to float away further. She is enjoying being tethered to him: the rusty chains of their swings bolted together close above their heads, his hand holding hers.

When they rock to stillness, she looks at Tommy only to find he is already watching her. And she is all at once embarrassed by her own cliché. She loves him. Not because she is tipsy, but because he is him and she is her, and in this moment, it feels as if that will always be enough. He runs a thumb across the back of her hand, and she is sure her heart actually beats faster, like the heroine of one of the Mills and Boon's Mamma hides in the drawer of her bedside table.

'The French have words for everything.' Tommy's eyes follow the path of an aeroplane high overhead. 'Everything important.' He smiles. 'I'll take you there one day. To France, I mean. Paris. We'll go to the galleries and drink proper wine by the Seine.'

'Will we indeed?' She laughs. 'When? With what money?'

His smile disappears. He twists in his swing to face her, the chains creaking.

'With the money I've been saving for us,' he says. 'When we're married.'

Rachel feels her stomach drop away from her. She is falling – crashing back into her own body. For a few seconds, she waits for his words to set solid between them. Then she nods.

'OK.' She lifts her free hand to his hair. 'I'll marry you.'

In the silence, she waits for him to backtrack. He will laugh, she thinks, and say that he never meant it to be a proposal – she takes things too seriously sometimes. Then she will have to laugh too and tell him she was joking, and they will kiss in that careless way that makes no promises.

Tommy doesn't laugh.

'When?' He leans into her hand. 'When will you marry me?'

She wants to say *anytime* and *now* and *yesterday*. But the wine is beginning to thrum in the back of her skull; the world beyond this scrubby field and this boy holding her hand in one corner of it is beginning to nudge at her. She slides her hand from his, their swings spinning away from each other.

'Mamma,' she says, then stops.

Tommy kicks off the ground, scattering dust over his penny loafers. 'We'll wait,' he says. 'You'll be eighteen soon. You'll finish school next summer. We'll do it then.'

'They won't allow it.' Rachel takes off too. 'We'll have to wait until I'm twenty-one. That's forever away.'

'We'll elope then.' He reaches out and catches her hand mid-swing, pulling her into his rhythm. 'I'll get you a ring, and then we'll go to Paris the day you finish school, and it'll be too late for anyone to say anything. Promise.'

They swing for a minute – too happy in their untested dream to be anything other than solemn.

'We'll be horribly poor, you know?' Tommy sighs. 'Artists are always poor.'

'We'll be terribly happy,' Rachel counters. 'Like in books.'

'If our life was a book, I would spend years struggling to win the patronage of a French aristocrat.'

Rachel grins at him. 'But you would win it. In the end.'

'Only if you died slowly and bravely of consumption in the attic bedroom of some backstreet boarding house.' Tommy smiles back. 'Isn't that how books work?'

'Not my sort of book.' Rachel tilts her head back again, closing her eyes against the bright autumn sunshine. 'In my book, people would be a little sad but a lot happy. They'd do only a little of the inevitable and a lot of the surprising.'

'Maybe your sort of book is the kind of romance where poor young lovers shelter from the rain in all the art galleries of Paris?' Tommy drags his feet, bringing them in to land. 'Perhaps they travel south to Spain or east in search of adventure? Maybe they spend their whole lives finding it.'

Rachel is floating again. Only, this time, Tommy is not anchoring her. He is bobbing beside her, waiting for the right breeze.

'Yes,' she says. 'Maybe they do.'

A History of Motherhood in Six Smiles

Smile One

She's too young, they say – it's only wind. But Katherine knows they're wrong. This gummy, uncontrolled gurgle is her reward for not having slept more than four hours a night for almost a month. This girl and this smile belong to her.

Smile Two

Katherine is first in line at the nursery door, seeking out Rachel's face in the crowd of toddlers cross-legged on the wooden floor. The other mothers press around her, and she fights the urge to shrink away, to brush them from her sleeves. She is not like them, not really – these women whose ration books and husband's wages won't quite allow them to stay home.

Rachel's eyes brim with relief when she sees Katherine. Her face breaks into sunshine. *Mamma is here. She has come back. She has not abandoned me to this strange new world.* Katherine unbuttons her gloves as Rachel toddles over, strokes her daughter's cheek, notes the new graze on her knee.

One day, Peter will get that promotion, Katherine tells herself. His salary will finally tip into three figures a year and, when it does, their daughter will never need this smile again.

Smile Three

Rachel fiddles with a thread hanging from one of the buttons. The dressing gown cord around her waist is loose already; Peter's oldest shirt gapes and bags around her.

At the front of the hall, the recorder group squeal their way to a stop. All the children look expectantly at Rachel, standing on one foot in the middle. She looks up, then down at the card in her hand. An expression of panic comes over her. She glances at her gesticulating teacher and then out towards the audience.

She sees Katherine and Peter, hand-in-hand on the front row. She sees them, and Katherine gives a little nod and smile. Rachel does the same – nod, smile – and squares her tiny shoulders. She takes a deep breath.

'Onceuponatime there was a woman called Mary and one day Angel Gabriel came to her and said youaregoingtohave-ababy and youmustcallhimJesus.'

Smile Four

When Katherine sees the photo, none of it matters anymore. All those weeks and months of worrying over the eleven-plus – what a waste. Under Rachel's gap-toothed grin, glowing down from the mantelpiece, Katherine doesn't care about any of it. She doesn't care that she didn't get to be one of the mothers parading along the High Street with parcels of new grammar-school uniform under her arm. Look at her – this girl in a navy gymslip and white blouse, Elmvale Secondary

Modern beret proudly on her head. Look at her. This girl can be anything she chooses to be. She can do anything at all.

Smile Five

There is a shout as the whistle blows. Eleven hockey sticks lift to the sky. The girls surround their captain in a screaming rush. Rachel, in the centre – so graceful, so long-legged and vibrant, Katherine almost doesn't recognise her – turns away and scans the sideline. When she sees Katherine, she raises her hand. Katherine raises hers in return.

Rachel's smile becomes uncertain, and she wavers – jogging a few steps towards Katherine, then pausing. Katherine shakes her head and waves her back to her team. They can have her now. Katherine's time will be later, when she plaits Rachel's wet hair for her as she eats hot-buttered crumpets in her nightdress, reliving every detail of the match for Peter. Katherine's time will come when she peeks through Rachel's door on her way to bed, pausing just long enough to watch the rise and fall of Rachel's chest, as she's done for fourteen years. Katherine's time is running out, but it is not gone yet.

Smile Six

Then there is this one.

This one is not instinct, or relief, or courage. It isn't the glow of youth or the ecstasy of success. Katherine doesn't know what it is.

Sometimes at dinner, Katherine asks Rachel a question and watches the ghost of this smile passing from her as she collects herself to answer. In the evening, as they sit in the front room, watching the black-and-white images of police crawling over Saddleworth Moor, Katherine turns to look at her daughter. She needs to reassure herself that she is still here, still belongs to her. But Rachel has gone. Her body is curled in the rocking chair, but her mind is somewhere else. She is not watching the screen but something behind it – beyond it. And she smiles this smile. And Katherine is so afraid that maybe she does know what it is after all.

She starts to rummage through Rachel's satchel when she is sleeping, checks under her pillow when she leaves for school. She finds nothing. She won't admit to herself the relief she feels when Rachel's sanitary belt is taken from the drawer.

Katherine doesn't understand this smile. She doesn't understand why it unsettles her. She only knows that this smile does not belong to her. She knows that this girl could be anything she chooses to be. This girl might do anything at all.

That Was the Week That Wasn't

There are a few days after Kenneth Tynan says That Horrid Word on the BBC for the first time when Rachel thinks that maybe things could be different. Later, people will say that he wasn't the first person after all – some drunk man already did it, or Miriam Margolyes said it on *University Challenge* years ago. Whatever. Kenneth Tynan says it, and for a week or so everybody waits to see what everybody else is going to think about it.

In that week, Rachel wonders if Maggie Marsh's Uncle Jack might be able to move into the same house as his good friend Mr Higgins, instead of spending another three decades living next door to each other, popping over for elevenses every morning, a nightcap every evening. She wonders if Jessica, who has a degree and her own house, will be allowed to go to the pictures with *that coloured chap* and still be invited over to her parents' for Sunday lunch. And she wonders whether she'll be able to show Mamma and Dad the ring Tommy bought her from the pawnbroker in Easthill.

Mamma won't be angry. Not this week. She'll cry happy-sad tears and talk about the son she never had. And Dad will give Tommy a stern lecture, then shake his hand and pour him a whisky. And Rachel will go into school and tell Maggie and all the others how she is going to get married as soon as their exams are over. She will marry but not settle down, not get pregnant straight away. She'll marry, and they'll head out on an adventure – husband and wife. Nomads. Because this week, anything is possible.

But a week after Kenneth Tynan says fuck on the BBC for the first time, Mary Whitehouse announces that she is forming the National Viewers' and Listeners' Association, and Mamma sits in front of the wireless saying things like *good for her* and *somebody needed to do something*. And Rachel pushes the little envelope further under her mattress and goes to bed without saying a word.

If You Really Love Her /
If He Really Loves You

You would've come to me first, surely? I'm her father. You should've asked my permission. What were you thinking? This isn't how it's done.

> *He would've gone to your father. He would've asked Daddy's permission. You should've told me about him, darling – I'm your mother! We should at least have met before he bought you that cheap ring. What were you thinking?*

You'd be happy to wait anyway, wouldn't you? She's seventeen, for goodness' sake – she's still at school. What's the hurry?

> *He'd be happy to wait until after your exams, at least. You're seventeen, for heaven's sake. I thought all girls wanted careers before husbands these days. You could make something of yourself – be a typist perhaps, or even a secretary to an important man. What's the hurry?*

You certainly wouldn't be talking all this nonsense about Paris. Do you even speak French? Well, there you are then. You're a part-time shop boy – how do you expect to make a life for my daughter in another country?

He would be more realistic. Paris? You're third from bottom in French at school. This isn't one of your Catherine Cookson's, darling. It might sound romantic, but you don't know what the French are like. And there's nothing romantic about starving.

You'd set these little drawings of yours aside. I'm sure they're decent efforts, but they won't put food on the table. There'll be no coal in the grate because you sell sketches at sixpence a time down the market. And what happens if you have a child?

He wouldn't be relying on doodles to provide for you. A doodler can't support a wife, let alone a child. Oh. You're not in trouble, are you, darling?

You would've talked things through rationally.

He would've got down on one knee.

You would've paid a call on her mother.

He would've spoken to your father.

You would've saved up for a house deposit.

He would've saved up for a better ring.

43

You would've got a proper job.

He would've got a proper job.

You'll give her a bit of space. You've called at the house three days in a row now – not once before she took that ring of yours. We aren't going to change our minds because you keep showing up. Give her time to think. If she's as in love with you as you say, it won't hurt, will it?

Why has he stopped coming round? Where's he been these last couple of days? He's left you to it, hasn't he? Is that the kind of man you want to marry?

Don't telephone for a bit. If you want us to respect her decision, then you need to give her time to think about it. Marriage isn't a game.

He'd at least have telephoned. Even if he doesn't have a telephone at home, there are telephone boxes, aren't there? He's treating it like a game.

Go to Paris. I'm serious. I've been thinking things through, and I'd like to make you an offer. If you think you can make a life in Paris, then do it. Show me you're serious. Move to Paris and get a job that means my girl wouldn't have to starve. I'll even help you on your way if you want.

He would live up to his promises. He'd get a job – prove to us he's serious, go somewhere with prospects.

I'll get you a ticket for the ferry. This weekend. I'm even prepared to give you enough money to cover lodgings for your first week. Then I'll give you two years to prove yourself. If, in two years, you've made a life for yourself out there and she still wants you, I'll let my daughter marry you. I won't make you wait until she's twenty-one.

You can give him a year, can't you? Let him go off for a year and prove himself. If he's back in twelve months and can provide for you, we'll all be much happier. If he's away more than that, then we'll know, won't we? He's either unable to provide or he's changed his mind, and it will be a lucky escape.

You'd respect my concerns as her father. Don't we both want what's best for her? Well, that's not this. There's nothing to stop you writing to her. People did it in the war, you know? More than two years sometimes. Men went off to do their duty, and they wrote letters. Make a man of yourself first.

He'd respect my concerns as your mother. I only want what's best for you. That's not a quick marriage to a man you barely know. You can always write to each other. In the war, people didn't see each other for years.

You'll understand why I can't let you marry her yet. You seem a decent young chap, but the time's not right. I'm only asking you for two years, Tommy. If you really love her, it will fly by. It's not forever, is it?

He'll understand why you can't keep his ring. We'll send it back to him, and he can make something of himself, then he can bring it back when he has. It's only a year, Rachel. If you really love him, it won't seem that long. It's not forever, is it?

Upon Your Return

And now here you are again. This street, this door, these net curtains – all made strange by your exile. This dryness in your mouth, this heartbeat in your throat, this deep breath. That face you have waited so long to see.

Here you are again. Only, this time, you will do it differently. This time you are not a shop boy who sells sketches in Fairfield Market on your day off. You might not quite be the artist you thought you'd be, but you are something more. You are a man. You are respectable. You have a job now, a savings account, a tiny house with a patch of garden in an area of Paris that, if not the best, is also not the worst. You speak French.

They asked you for two years. Rachel's parents sent you away for two years to make the life you'd promised their daughter. And it is one year and eleven months and three days. Seven hundred and two days since you opened the envelope and the ring you'd found in the pawnshop window fell spinning at your feet, a one-line note fluttering next to it.

I can't. Not yet. I'm sorry. R x

Six words. Six funereal drumbeats. Then the x – not a kiss, but an execution, a crossing out of everything you had before. Being young and poor had tricked you into thinking that love could make youth and poverty an irrelevance. You hadn't believed in the face of your feelings – of *Rachel's* feelings – her parents could possibly say no. And it was not a no. Not really. It was a not yet. You had the ticket to Paris; you had the promise of her dad. When you had come to say goodbye to Rachel and found that her mother had taken her to visit a distant cousin, her dad had clapped you on the back. He'd smiled at you. He'd wished you well.

And now here you are again. Not quite two years, perhaps, but near enough. You would've carried out the full sentence if Rachel had answered your last two letters. But six months of silence has made you uneasy. Has she moved – her new address gone astray? Is she ill?

You hadn't written often. Phone calls from France were beyond your means. Postage was beyond your means too at first, but you did what you could – a letter only every two or three months, saving every franc possible. Her replies always came typed, hand-signed with that single R. You imagined her, straight-backed at the typewriter her parents had bought her when she started at secretarial college, practising her touch-typing as she wrote. You could tell from her formality, her restrained brevity, that her parents were reading the letters too. And so you were restrained as well. Nothing more than *I miss you*, a sole *I can't wait to see you again*. You didn't tell her of the rats in your first lodgings, nor the damp in your second. You avoided details of your first job, sweeping the fag ends and broken glass from the floor of a downmarket bistro. But, imagining her mother scanning the lines over Rachel's shoulder, you told her of your house. You told her when you had enough savings to pay the month's rent in advance and when your French became good enough to be offered a job as a junior clerk. In return, she told you about college and the weather and hoped you were well. You had to make do with that. It was like the war, you told yourself. Just as her father had said it would be: brief letters, waiting for each other. It was romantic, wasn't it?

And now here you are again. Your hat in your hand, the ring – a new ring from a real jeweller this time – in your pocket. The front door opening wide to reveal Rachel's mother in her house dress, eyebrows raised.

'Thomas Granger, Ma'am,' you say, in case she has forgotten. 'I wonder if I might speak with Rachel.'

'Rachel?' She glances down the road as if unwilling for any neighbours to see you, even though you borrowed Alain's best suit. 'I'm afraid she isn't here.' She hesitates, and in that hesitation, you see that she does remember you, only too well. 'Rachel's on honeymoon.'

No. That's not right. And yet, you already see it. Of course. Rachel's letters were not the words of someone afraid of saying too much; they were the words of someone who has too little to say. It's too late. If Rachel had been engaged, it would have been late, but not too late. You might have pleaded with her, resurrected your dream of adventure. Honeymoon is too late. Another man has stood at this door before you with a ring in his pocket.

The woman in the doorway gives you a pitying smile. 'I'm sorry, Thomas.'

'No. That's... marvellous.' You are already backing down the path. 'Wonderful news. Please tell her... tell her...' What? That you waited? That you were that stupid? That you've barely drawn anything for two years because you needed her even more than you needed your art? 'Wish her the very best of luck from me, will you?'

You know she won't.

And so here you are again. Walking away without Rachel.

And so tomorrow you will go back to Paris and resign from the job that means nothing without her.

And so you will give notice on the house she will never live in.

And so you will take your pens and inks and disappear into the life you offered to leave for her. And maybe, if you travel enough miles and sleep with enough women and drink enough beer, one day you will be able to draw something other than her face.

No Lawful Impediment

Francis is a good man.

Francis loves her.

Francis makes her laugh.

Francis will still think she is beautiful when her nose is dripping or her hair needs cutting or dark, musty circles form under the arms of her blouse on hot summer days.

Francis knows her well enough to have stopped bringing flowers every Friday night when he comes to have dinner with her parents, and to bring a paperback from the second-hand bookshop on the corner of Gargrave Street instead.

Francis is waiting in this church – this half-full church that Mamma chose because she liked the ceiling painted with fat angels trailing streamers of grapes. He is waiting at the end of that aisle, buttonholed with early primroses. He isn't waiting to get it over with. He isn't waiting for the show her parents have spent too much money on to start. He is waiting for her. He only wants these iron-studded doors to open and to see her – to offer up all he has: stability, acceptance, his home, his name. He wants to hold it out to her in the jewelled light of the windows above the altar and see her claim it as her own. That is all he is asking from her: nothing and everything. For as long as they both shall live.

On the steps outside, Rachel can feel her own name slipping from her – rolling down her veil and along the lace train, puddling in the churchyard behind. Even now, she could claim it back. She could pull her arm from her father's and gather those letters up and run with them in shoes that are a little too tight and a lot too high. She could run all the way home, all the way into a different life, all the way to Paris.

But Francis is a good man. Francis loves her and makes her laugh and thinks she's beautiful and is waiting for her here. So when her father gives her the are-you-sure-you're-sure look it's his duty to give, and when the ushers put their hands on the door handles and watch for her signal, and when her cousin Pam holds out the bouquet for her to take, Rachel nods and leaves the puddle to dry in the weak winter sun.

A Bigger Splash

'Filthy lucre,' he slurs, slopping beer onto the sticky table. 'That's what it's all about for those big shots. Fucking money.'

You roll your eyes at the women at the next table. *I'm not like him*, you try to convey. *We're not all like this.*

Rupert lights another fag and takes a long drag. 'Not us, Tommy. Proper art. That's what we'll be about.'

'Keep your voice down.' You pull his beer away from the table edge. 'Not everybody wants to listen to you banging on about Hockney.'

'Hockney.' He shakes his head, takes another swig of beer. 'Where's that card you keep in your sketchbook.' He smacks you on the shoulder, a little too hard. 'Get it out, Tommo.'

You don't want to get it out. It cost you five pence, that card. That's five fags, a quarter of a pint of beer. You don't want Rupert to get his hands on it. Not when he's already half-cut at 6 p.m.

'Get it out,' he says again, louder this time. 'I'll show you why it's shit.'

More to stop him shouting than anything else, you pull the postcard from the back of your book. You put it on the table between you, but you don't take your hand from it.

'Look at it.' Rupert waves his fag around, spilling ash down his velvet jacket. 'What's so good about that?'

You look. The painting pictured on the card is dominated by horizontals. Turquoise water separated from brilliant sky by a strip of earthy pink, a low-slung building, flat-topped and exotic in between. From the front right corner of the picture, a diving board juts out at an unexpected angle as if you could step out onto it into that bright Californian light.

Rupert watches you. 'Go on. Tell me that Hockney's a genius.'

You nod slowly. 'Hockney's a genius.'

He sighs and snatches the card from under your fingers. 'Excuse me.' He holds it up to the neighbouring women. 'What do you think of this?'

'What is it?' The nearest woman takes it from him.

'A painting,' Rupert says. '*A Bigger Splash*. Do you like it?'

She shrugs and hands it back. 'It's nice.'

'See.' Rupert is triumphant. 'Nice. Three years at the RCA – do you know they changed the rules about graduating just for him? – three years, and he's producing stuff that's *nice*. And getting paid a bloody fortune for it, I bet.'

You want to argue. You want to draw his attention to the raw edges of the canvas, to point at the splash in the centre of the picture. Any other artist would've cheated to make that splash. Hell, *you* would've cheated if you'd painted it. How do you make a splash look authentic? You splash the paint on, of course. Not Hockney. He painted it on by hand with fine brushes. Two weeks it took him. And you want to tell Rupert how much you love it: how you love that the person who's made the splash is hidden in the depth of the pool, invisible to the viewer; how the picture makes you feel as if somewhere there is warmth and energy and something bigger than your dingy London digs and an art school packed with people like you, who will never be a Hockney.

There's no point saying any of that, though. Rupert will never get it.

'We'll do it properly,' he's saying. 'We'll paint *real* real life. Ordinary people doing ordinary stuff. None of this glamorous shit. We'll get old men playing chess on street corners and red-faced mothers scrubbing their laundry in metal tubs.'

This is what Rupert thinks being poor is, you realise: something Dickensian with a smattering of *Steptoe and Son*. It's fingerless gloves and cheery songs round the only fire. It's simple but hearty stews containing mysteries such as scrag end. It's not bob-a-jobbing all weekend so Dad can pay the electric or eating spaghetti hoops for tea five days in a row.

Rupert is at least committed to his ideal of poverty. He has stage-managed getting himself thrown out of home and is drinking away the last of his money with gusto. He will make himself a true Starving Artist. And although you're happy to help with the drinking, your heart isn't fully with him. Whereas Rupert is committed to being poor, you are merely resigned to it. Being skint is not your badge of honour. You wouldn't mind seeing what rich is like.

With a clumsy sweep of his hand, Rupert sloshes beer into his lap. He jumps up, swearing.

'Gentlemen.' The landlord looks over. 'None of that, if you don't mind.'

'Time to go, Rupe.'

'Already?' He flings an arm around your shoulders. 'It's not even dark.'

'We'll go to the offie on the way home,' you promise. 'We can sneak a bottle of something into digs in that ridiculous coat of yours.'

'I like the way you think, Tommo.' He leans down and plucks something from the table. 'Don't forget your precious card.'

You look at that splash again in the smoky light of the pub. And you wonder how it's possible to capture something so transient, so transparent.

'It *is* ordinary life,' you say. 'In California, it's normal to have a pool.'

But Rupert is already at the door – the burn of the pound note in his pocket, propelling him onwards. You should go with him – make sure he buys the wine you like instead of the half-bottle of absinthe he thinks he should be drinking. And so you slip the card back into your sketchbook for the next time you need it – for the next time you need to know that somewhere an artist is making some money, that somewhere people swim in sunshine, and that somewhere, deep beneath it all, there is a man waiting to surface.

Expectation

Maggie is going to have a PhD, and Rachel is going to have a baby. They share the news over éclairs at the Hawkins Tea Rooms when Maggie is back home for Christmas. She looks at Rachel's half-grown belly, and Rachel looks at her half-gone cigarette, and they smile polite smiles.

Maggie will be the first person from Elmvale Secondary Modern ever to get a Dr in front of her name. Mrs Croft has already asked her to give out the prizes next Speech Day, even though she has three years to go before she gets it. Rachel is not the first to work in the typing pool at Austin Cooks, nor to have a baby. She's not even the first in their class. But she is the first out of her and Maggie.

Maggie's mother is worried that Maggie is leaving it too late to find a husband, and then what use will all her learning be? Maggie rolls her eyes as she tells Rachel about it, fiddling with the hem of the Twiggy dress that's too short for a house-wife to wear but would be just Rachel's colour.

Rachel's mother has decided Rachel's having a boy. She has knitted a hat and two blue jackets already.

'What's it like?' Maggie says.

'What's it like?' Rachel asks.

And they decide that when Maggie is fifty and doesn't need to, she'll marry a millionaire, and that when Rachel's children are grown up, Rachel will do something clever and fabulous. And they lick cream from their fingers and don't quite look each other in the eye.

At First Sight

She waits for the rush. Rachel has been promised a rush. As she looks down at the squashed, purple shape in her arms, she waits. And the other two people in the room watch her waiting.

This is how it has been sold to her. There will be pain, of course, but then there will be the rush. It's what the nice lady at the antenatal class has implied. It's what her friends have told her as they hitched their cotton-soft, milk-fat babies onto their hips. It's like nothing else on earth, they said. Unbelievable. Overwhelming. You look down, and you see your baby, and you get a rush of love like you've never known before.

Francis leans over her. 'Isn't he beautiful?' He has tears in his eyes, his voice low and filled with new notes. Francis never cries.

Rachel looks again. The baby's head is long and domed from his uneasy passage out of her. Patches of vernix colour his skin. His unfocussed eyes are staring up at her, face wrinkled as if he is considering whether to cry again.

'Yes,' she says. 'Beautiful.'

'What shall we call him?' Francis kisses her sweat-soaked hair. 'You did all the work – you should choose.'

She thinks of the names on their shortlist: kings and saints and great-grandfathers. She doesn't know which one to pick. Which collection of letters should they choose for their son? It seems too early to label him.

'How about Henry?'

Francis beams. 'Yes. He looks like a Henry, don't you think? Henry Francis Flynn. I like that.'

'My nephew's called Henry,' the midwife chips in. 'A good solid name that.'

Rachel is still shaking. The adrenaline needed to get her through the last few hours of her fifteen-hour labour is still running wild in her veins. She wants a bath. She wants a cup of tea. She wants to be on her own to process the strange, agonising thing that has just happened to her. She wants – so desperately wants – to feel the rush. She doesn't want to have failed at this first test of motherhood.

Francis perches on the edge of the bed beside her and slides an arm around her shoulders. She is grateful to him for this. He has been there every minute of the labour – he saw her waters break and her bowels open and heard her scream through every one of the last six hours of contractions. And despite all that, he is still prepared to put his arm around her sodden nightdress and squeeze her tight to him, one hand stroking the dark hair of their new son.

'Shall we try a feed?' the midwife says.

She doesn't wait for a reply. Of course Rachel will want to feed him. Never mind her blood-stained thighs and salt-stained forehead, she is his mother – of course she will want to provide.

Henry looks up suspiciously as the midwife helps Rachel manoeuvre him into position. As Rachel's nipple brushes his lips, he opens his mouth – suddenly, frantically aware that he needs something. He clamps to her with a grunt of possession. The midwife bustles out of the room, scooping up the pile of stained sheets from the doorway.

'You were amazing,' Francis says to her as soon as they are alone. 'What you just did.' He shakes his head. 'Wow.'

They watch their son together for a few minutes until the midwife calls from the kitchen to say she can't find the tea, and Francis hurries off to be efficient.

Rachel looks at Henry. His eyes are shut, cheeks round. He is making little gulping, snuffly noises. She decides to try his name.

'Hello, Henry.'

When he doesn't respond, she tries her new name as well.

'I'm Mummy.'

He opens his deep-blue eyes, and they become still as they settle on her face. He swallows once more and then allows her nipple to slide out of his mouth. She feels absurdly as if he is assessing her – measuring her up for a role she has applied for without any qualifications or experience. And she can't tell what conclusion he is coming to.

'I'll try,' she tells him. 'I'll try my best.'

His face crumples again, and she thinks he is going to scream – to sound the alarm that this woman has been allowed to bring him into the world without any vetting procedure, without anybody asking her whether her insides go gooey when she sees a baby, or whether she is the type of person to feel a rush of love when one is required of her. Then his eyes slowly close again. He is asleep.

Something stirs inside Rachel's exhausted, torn body. It is not a rush. It is the slow-moving unfurling of a quick-growing vine. It binds itself around her, tugging on her edges, taking everything that was before this moment and slowly dragging it away. As she looks down at Henry's sleeping face for the first of a hundred thousand times, she feels it creeping over her heart, pulling the corners wide. No, it is not a rush. But it is something.

Anabelle

She is the sort of girl your mother didn't warn you about: well-mannered, educated, funny. Beautiful too. Not your type at all.

She is your O-level English teacher's worst nightmare – all those nondescript words you were told not to put into your essays, but that describe her perfectly. She is nice. She is lovely.

She is not the sort of girl who comes to events like this – back-alley galleries filled with tiny pictures from unknown, unknowable artists barely out of school. She doesn't fit in here, in her just-down-from-the-country dress. She can't possibly appreciate gritty, impoverished art. She shouldn't be here.

And yet, she is.

You've not looked at a girl in six years – not for anything more serious than sex – so it should be safe to go over to her, to stand only inches away and watch as she traces the lines of your drawing with a manicured fingertip. It shouldn't matter to you that she has chosen your work – not the oils and acrylics of your friends, but your pen and ink drawings washed over with blocks and swathes of watercolour. She is not your type, and you cannot be hers, so it should be safe for your fingers to join hers on the paper.

She is probably the sort of girl who will make you change for her. She will probably stop you smoking and drinking and swearing. And when you find that she has no intention of stopping you doing any of those things, you will find that you want to stop them anyway. When you are with her, you will never feel as if you are an adventure to ease her ennui. You are not the scandal to get her noticed in better circles than yours. And if she doesn't understand when you talk of meat paste and dripping, or tinned fruit with evaporated milk on Sundays, it won't matter because she will understand why you used that particular shade of red and why you have to stop on the corner of the park when the light is hitting the row of sweet chestnuts at just that angle.

She is the sort of girl whose quiet questions – all received pronunciation and lowered eyes – will flummox you into clumsy answers. She is the sort of girl your mother didn't warn you about on those last few nights as she lay coughing by the gas fire, cramming a lifetime of advice into your too-young head. She is a girl with no wild corners, no sharp edges, no hard memories. Not your type at all.

Wildflowers: A History

She says the names to herself as she walks up the lane, even though he is not here to listen. *Tansy. Feverfew. Toadflax.* If she lets herself, she will be able to hear his voice. *Look, Mummy, musk mallow!* She will be able to feel the weight of him bouncing along on her back, wellies drumming against her thighs.

They have walked for miles along these leaf-dappled lanes – hundreds of miles, she supposes – with Henry asleep in his pram at first, then riding high in the carrier on her back. When the visitors had stopped coming with their Mothercare gift sets and casseroles for the freezer, she had needed this. On those grey-tinged mornings when that fierce, surprising love was still not enough to make her forget who she'd been before she'd been his mother, she had found herself in the rhythm of her footsteps.

At the gate, she stops to admire the slender petals of the woody nightshade nodding over the stream beyond the wall. She will show Henry this. On the way back from school, she will lift him up, and they will play their game where they both have to make up a new name for it, and even though she will think of something poetic – *afternoon star*, perhaps, *mother's joy* – and he will call it something like *pointy purple yellow face*, they will both agree that he has won.

They'd learned the flowers together. When he was babbling his first words, she was teaching herself to distinguish hedge parsley from wild carrot, cat's-ear from rough hawkbit. She'd say the names aloud as they walked, and it made her feel better. Their walks were for his education, not her escape. She didn't have to feel guilty that sometimes – just for one minute, just for one deep breath – she wished for a few more inches between them. How she loved him; how she ached to see him fly a little further from her side.

In the kitchen, she drops the shopping bags and flicks the switch on the kettle. Her eyes wander to the clock above the sink. What is he doing now? Maybe he is sitting at one of those tiny blue tables, learning to distinguish b from d, 2 from 5. His hair will be dishevelled, his tongue poking out as he follows the dots with his HB pencil. And when she picks him up, he will have grown another few inches. In the three weeks since he started school, his limbs have grown impossibly long, his horizons dazzlingly wide.

This growth has always caught her unawares; ounces and inches appearing in a trickle or a thunderclap. Last spring, he had all at once become too heavy for her back. Their walks had circled closer to home as he had bumbled along beside her. In the far field, he would run ahead, aeroplane wings spread wide, engine noises spluttering into giggles as she chased him, caught him by the hands, spun him until they were both dizzy. They would stop to say hello to the sheep or to look up a flower in the handbook Francis had bought her from Foyles last time he was in London. If the flower had more than one name, she would read them all, and Henry would choose his favourite. *Lords-and-Ladies* or *Jack-in-the-pulpit*? *Cow parsley* or *Queen Anne's Lace*? If he didn't like any of them, they would give it a new one – a name just for them.

At the school gate, he comes running to her, satchel flapping. She asks how he is, did he have a nice day, what has he been doing in the six hours and forty-one minutes they have been apart. He shrugs. *Nothing much.*

On the walk home, she teases from him a little more of the nothing much: phonics and finger-painting. When they reach their gate, she tugs him to a stop, lifts him up, pulls back a wayward leaf to show him her discovery.

'Look, Henry, what do you think that is?'

He glances at the flower then to her face. And the look he gives her is one he has been giving her more often of late. It is as if he has glimpsed something he hadn't realised was there. He has seen her, the stranger beneath her skin. He has remembered once more that he and she are not the same person after all.

'It's a purple flower, Mummy.' He wriggles from her arms and climbs onto the bottom bar of the gate to release the latch. 'Can I have a snack?'

A purple flower. He is right, of course.

She watches him run down the track to the back door. How she loves him, how she aches to see him fly a little further from her side. She pauses just long enough to touch one fragile petal. *Woody nightshade* or *bittersweet*? Then she begins to chase after him. And she knows that however fast she runs, however far she stretches, she will not catch him this time.

Bienvenue à L'Hôtel

Welcome to the Ritz Paris. We hope you enjoy your stay. We pride ourselves on providing you with every modern comfort a discerning gentleman can expect, so please don't hesitate to ask for anything you may need. We look forward to welcoming you for a cocktail in the bar or to our world-famous *L'Espadon* to experience the finest cuisine.

As an artist, you will no doubt be fascinated by the *Belle Époque* artwork that you see around our hotel. You will be inspired and, perhaps, a little depressed, by the craftwork, by the opulence, by the things other people have created and you have not. On the first morning of your honeymoon, you will look out of your double windows onto the gilded façade of the *Palais Garnier*, and you will wonder how you have got here. How is it that you are standing in one of the finest suites in one of the finest hotels in the world? You will think of all the people who have slept and drunk and dined here – Hemingway and F. Scott Fitzgerald, countless queens and film stars – and you will feel giddy, frightened even. Your wife – whom you are not yet used to calling your wife – will slip back into the room and tell you that she is almost sure the old woman she passed in the lobby is Greta Garbo, and isn't that too marvellous?

Please note the attention to detail in our decor – marble fireplaces, golden swan taps. Bathe in the romance of the Ritz Paris experience. What better surroundings could there be for your first days of marriage? What better way to highlight the stark difference between your history and hers? Note how she speaks to the *maître d'* in a way that is classy: superior but not snobby. See how she is used to these places. Marvel at how this woman – with her incredible face and that astonishing trust fund – has chosen you. In the small hours of the morning, lie awake under our finest linen sheets and sumptuous down duvets, wondering why her parents put up no objection to the match. Why did they put aside your obvious lack of money, breeding and commercial success? Is the Struggling Artist For a Son-in-Law story an interesting dinner party fallback? Are you an act of charitable patronage? Let it needle at you a little; let it pluck at the edges of your doubt.

May we suggest taking time to enjoy an afternoon sweet in the *Grand Jardin*? As you sit under the linden trees and take tiny bites of your exquisite pastry, you can watch the sunlight on your wife's face and wonder how you might capture it in pen and ink. And when she asks you if this is what you wanted when you told her of your dream to honeymoon in Paris, you will press her fingers to your lips and say you never imagined anything like this.

We are sure you will find our hotel the ideal location from which to explore the delights of Paris. When you return from your tour of flying buttresses and the endless boutiques of the *Triangle D'Or*, perch on your satin and brocade sofa and try to listen to your wife. Concentrate on the names of all the castles and cousins she is planning to visit with you. Don't think about those enticing glimpses of back alleys – the swish and colour of ordinary lives.

On your last evening, as you sip your final martini on the terrace, your wife will offer you a penny for your thoughts. When you don't answer, she will laugh and ask if you are thinking how lucky you are to have such a beautiful and intelligent wife. And you will laugh too and look at her good, kind face, and promise yourself that the next time she asks that question, you won't have to lie.

An Inheritance

It's odd how everyone feels the need to say it, Rachel thinks. *Henry is so like his father.* Teachers, doctors, mums at the school gate – they all feel the need to tell Rachel what she knows better than any of them, what she sees across the table every morning at breakfast.

These are the things Henry takes from Francis:

Blue eyes.

Dirty-blond curls and a dimple in his left cheek.

A nose that is a little long for his face, set above a serious mouth with an unexpected smile.

He likes cricket and knowing how things work, and he is a little taller than most other eight-year-olds.

When talking about something that hasn't quite gone right, he will end with, 'Ho-hum,' and a deep sigh.

He is excellent at maths and mediocre at music.

He is kind.

He will never be an artist.

Nobody ever tells Rachel that Henry is at all like her. Nobody seems to hear the notes of her that whistle from Henry as he dashes past or see the tiny flecks of her scattered through him.

Even her own mother can't see it. And yet, these are the things Henry has taken from Rachel:

Long fingers.

A tendency to put his head on one side when thinking.

A love of Marmite and cottage cheese on toast.

He has taken away the firmness of her belly and her apathy towards politics, and her ability to make small talk with adults.

He has pilfered pieces of her to fuel his growth – splinters and shards she didn't realise had gone until too late: the smoothness of the skin around her eyes; her tolerance for late nights; the insidious idea that she'll probably be a good mother.

He has snatched hours of sleep from under her eyelids.

He has taken her fears for the future and tossed them back to her, swollen far beyond the end of her lifespan. Will there be nuclear war in fifty years? Will fossil fuels run out in sixty? Will Henry's grandchildren have clean air to breathe eighty years from now?

He has torn a piece from the centre of her heart and grown himself around it, like an oak swallowing a fence wire as it thickens. She can still feel it sometimes – that dull ache in her chest – when watching him ask to join a football game or when he stands up to speak his lines in the end-of-term assembly.

There were times when she thought he might take all of her – that he would chip away at her until there was nothing left. But she has found instead that as he takes, she takes too. He has taken away a dozen different paths she might have walked without him, but he has given her another path to set her feet on instead. He has filled her with tiny, powerful magic. There is the silver sliver of stretch mark curving under her belly button like a smile or a snake. There is her new knowledge of the relative sizes of dinosaurs and how hover-crafts work. She has taken from him the excuse to examine iridescent beetles that cross their path, and to jump the last two stairs, and to rock on a swing singing The Everly Brothers' hits.

Whilst Henry was expanding her fears (choking, cot death, speeding cars), he was shaping her hopes as well. For how could the world fail to be safe in the hands of a boy who rescues bees from his paddling pool and plants apple pips with sure expectancy? He has given her hope. And, more than anything, he has given her moments like this, when she sits at the breakfast table and listens to the ceaseless outpouring of his brilliant, quirky mind and all the inventions and adventures it offers. Moments like this, when as she listens to him, she catches Francis's eye and Francis smiles and says, 'He gets this from you, you know.'

A Matter of Time

She hovers in the doorway, tray pressed close to her belly. She doesn't speak. And you hate how you have done this to her. You've never raised a hand to her, rarely raised your voice and yet your jitters, your frustrations have made her nervous of you – nervous of how she might find you in here. You hate your need to overcompensate every time.

'Hello, beautiful.' You lay down your pen in the pool of light flooding your desk from the Anglepoise lamp and push your chair back with a scrape of metal on concrete.

Anabelle hurries across the studio and looks for somewhere to put the tray. 'I made cake,' she says. 'Jam sponge.'

You clear a stack of preliminary sketches from the top of the paint cupboard and take the tray from her. 'Perfect.'

She removes a heap of paint tubes from the only other chair and stacks them back in the cupboard, each in its place: cerulean, burnt umber, alizarin crimson. When you are both settled, she takes a deep breath and then doesn't ask what she's desperate to ask.

'I sold one.' You rescue her from her indecision. 'Sixty pounds.'

'Wonderful!' She leans over and kisses you. 'Well done, darling. Which one?'

'The one of your dad reading his newspaper in the Italian Garden.'

'I knew you'd sell that one. Daddy will be so pleased it's one of him.'

Anabelle cuts the cake with the silver cake knife you got her for your fourth wedding anniversary. She is proud of this – her status as a woman who bakes cakes. The money she brought into this marriage was plenty enough to buy Sonning Cottage on the edge of the Great Park – a house that only a Queen would consider a cottage – but she hasn't plunged you into an *Upstairs, Downstairs* world. She has a part-time house-keeper who does the toilets and scrubs the oven and runs a hoover round twice a week, but Anabelle herself has learned to garden and to cook and to feel just a little superior to the rest of her family who can't do either of those things. She is a proud 1950s housewife, a quarter of a century too late.

'Daddy is still keen to help you, you know.' She doesn't look at you as she says it. 'Any time you want help then...'

You don't want help. You want to not have help so much. If your drawings are to mean anything to anybody, it must be through talent, not nepotism. You glance round at the stacks of your talent heaped in the corners. Perhaps in another decade, if you are still only selling a dozen drawings a year in the market or at third-rate art shows, you will put aside your principles, but not yet.

'He's not doing it because it's you.' Anabelle passes you a slice of cake, drops two sugars into your tea with tiny tongs. 'He has his reputation to think of. If he patronised you only because of me, then people would talk; he'd lose a lot of respect. He wouldn't do that, Tommy. He really does believe in you.'

Maybe this is true. You'd like it to be true, and not just kind-ness. Because he is kind. Curiously, confusingly kind, in a way that makes you grateful and resentful in almost equal measure. People with so much money aren't meant to be kind. They're meant to ask you about your parentage and prospects and roll their eyes when you get some social nicety wrong. They aren't meant to babysit for their gardeners and whisper to you between courses at family weddings so you know which cutlery to use.

When you'd first met Anabelle's parents, you'd been all ready to list your ten O-levels and three A-levels – scrape together a curriculum vitae of anything that might work in your favour. They hadn't even asked. Did Anabelle love you? Were you going to be faithful to Anabelle? Well then. They'd even liked your drawings. They'd said so, anyway. So in another, say, five years, it wouldn't be so bad to allow your renowned art collector of a father-in-law to give you a hand up, would it? Maybe even in three years. That wouldn't be cheating.

In between bites of sponge, you fiddle with the edges of a rough sketch. It's of Anabelle collecting dahlias in her wicker trug. A snapshot of the life that is yours now: English country gardens, boxes on opening nights, silver cake knives and real china cups.

'I don't mind what you do with your art if you're happy.' Anabelle squeezes lemon into her Earl Grey. 'But I know it's brilliant. Daddy does too. So if you're *not* happy, don't be too proud to accept some help, will you?'

You look down at the paper version of her and wonder what you would be drawing if she hadn't been the daughter of Sir Gervase and Lady Beatrice but just some girl you met at a bus stop. Anabelle at a tiny kitchen table mixing up packets of Smash, perhaps? Anabelle in her Safeway pinafore tying up her hair for work? Maybe not Anabelle at all.

She is still looking at you. So you reach over and touch the tiny swell of her belly.

'Give me eighteen months,' you say. 'When our baby has its first birthday. If I'm not world-famous by then, I'll talk to your dad.'

She smiles and lifts your hand to her lips. 'You won't need to,' she says. 'People will realise what they're missing soon.' She offloads your cup and saucer onto the desk and picks up the tray. 'I'll leave you to it.'

Eighteen months. You've said it now. You've given yourself a deadline: success in eighteen months. You sit alone in your studio, surrounded by unwanted drawings awash with hopeful colours. Eighteen months you said. And you look at the piles of blank paper, the ink bottles, the tubes of paint. And you wish you'd said six.

Way Out West Somewhere

Henry is too high already. From the far end of the field, Rachel watches him climb. His legs have grown long and tanned through the lazy weeks of summer, and they feel their way through the limbs of the old oak with an ease that catches Rachel's breath.

'Laika – here!' Rachel whistles and waits for Laika to come wriggling under the fence. As they cross the grass, she can feel the words crowding into her mouth: *too high; stop there; get down; be careful.* She presses her lips together.

'Mum, look.' Henry peers down at her. 'I can see the new barn from here. Come up.'

Laika has found a stick that is nearly as big as her and is bouncing around Rachel's feet.

'Daft animal.' Rachel throws the stick as far as she can, then hauls herself up to the bottom branch. It isn't as easy as she remembers.

'I fell out of a tree once.' She looks up at her son. 'When I was about your age.'

'Did you?' Henry looks impressed, and Rachel feels an absurd wiggle of pleasure. 'Did you break your leg?'

'Afraid not.' She sits down, back against the trunk, and kicks off her shoes. 'I got concussion, though. Woke the next day with an awful headache – was off school for a week.'

'Cool!'

If she stretches her left arm now, she would be able to reach his dangling right leg. She would be able to cup her hand around that skinny calf, feeling the weight of him, the shape of him, the familiar strangeness of the boy who is half her. She doesn't.

'Why did you fall?' he says, full of pity for an inferior tree-climber.

'I leaned back too far trying to spot a dog in a spaceship. I got dizzy.'

'You didn't.'

Rachel shrugs. 'I did, actually.'

'A dog in a spaceship?'

'Yep.'

Henry thinks about this for a few seconds. 'Did you see it?'

'No.' She doesn't tell him what she didn't learn for years afterwards – that the dog was almost certainly dead already by then.

Across the field, Laika is lying in the sun chewing her stick – a content brown and white heap of spaniel. At five years old, she is still the puppy she had been when Francis had brought her home. She was supposed to have been a Christmas present for Henry, but Rachel knew Laika was really for her. Laika was a gap-filler, a space-taker-upper, something else that was a little too loud and a little too wild; someone else to name and to love.

In the tree above her, Henry has hauled himself to his feet. He wraps his hands around the trunk and leans backwards. Further and further he goes, swaying slightly as if daring history to repeat itself. All the warnings poised on Rachel's tongue shift and nudge at each other. Yet she still holds them back because when he glances down, she spots that expression on his face – the one she has no business taking from him.

The first time she saw Henry look like this, he was three. They were standing on Brighton Pier watching the waves beat against it, a band of rain approaching them from the horizon. The second time he was five and running down a grassy hill towards her outstretched arms. He was running a little too fast, on the edge of losing control. She has seen the same expression many times since, and although it is something different every time, every time it is the same. This is what her son's face looks like when he is on the cusp of something unstoppable, something wild.

'Where do you think that plane's going?' Henry says.

He pulls his centre of gravity in towards the trunk, and Rachel draws another breath. She scans the sky and spots the far-off contrail heading out towards the Atlantic.

'Way out west somewhere,' she says. 'Canada, perhaps. Or California.'

'I'm going to Canada one day.' Henry snaps a splintered twig from its branch. 'And California. I'm going to go everywhere and see everything in the whole world.'

'Are you?' Rachel looks away. 'Will you take me with you?' She is careful to make it sound like a joke.

'You'll be too old.' Henry examines the branches above him and then heaves himself up to the next one. 'By the time I'm grown-up, you'll be ancient.'

'I'm thirty-two, Henry. When you turn eighteen, I'll be forty.'

He shrugs. 'Exactly.'

Rachel sighs and drops barefoot into the grass. Spotting the movement, Laika leaps to her feet and races over, ears flapping. Rachel crouches to pet her, half-heartedly attempting to wrestle the stick from her jaws. Laika is still winning when a flurry of acorns pepper them from above and catch her on the nose. She yelps, and at the same time, Henry yelps too.

Even as she is still straightening up, still turning back to the tree, Rachel's arms are ready. She is ready to catch, ready to crumple beneath the weight of him. But Henry isn't falling. The toes of his right foot are resting on a knot in the trunk, his left ones sweeping the air to find a hold. His body is wrapped round a branch, suspended from his armpits.

'Mum, help me.' It's his not-quite-panicking voice, the Mum-can-fix-this voice he so rarely needs anymore. 'I can't see where to put my feet.'

Rachel scans the tree. There are two branches he could reach. If he shifts to the left, he could find a toehold and lower himself down onto a sturdy bough. If he shifts to the right and stretches a bit further, he could reach up for the next branch. He can come down, or he can climb a little higher.

'Mum?'

Rachel looks up at this boy and, just for a second, she hesitates. She stands with her arms spread wide, and she waits to hear which words her tongue will choose to say.

All the People You Speak to on the Opening Night of Your First Exhibition

Here he is. The man himself. See all these people? Told you didn't I, m'boy? Been wanting to arrange this for years. I knew we'd get here one day. I'm never wrong about an artist – especially when he's married to m'daughter. Where's your glass? Waiter! Champagne for the artist!

~

The nice woman at the front desk let me use her phone, darling. I got through to the babysitter, and she said the girls went to sleep like a dream, so that's good, isn't it? Gosh. Look at all these people. They've all come to see your drawings. Isn't that too marvellous?

~

God. Look at all this. What a bloody show, hey? Loving the free booze. Well done, Tommo, old pal – one of us has made a big splash at last. Don't suppose I'll be having a grand opening any time soon. No... no hard feelings; I'm bloody chuffed for you. Must be nice having a father-in-law to pull all the strings. Not that you don't deserve it, I'm not saying that. Most of it's good stuff. I've been doing some similar pieces myself, actually. Just got to get me a rich wife now, hey? Bloody chuffed for you, pal. Bloody chuffed.

~

Graham told me this was *the* place to be tonight, but gawd have you seen the stuff? That picture that's meant to be the centre of the whole show – *Anabelle in the Grand Jardin* – I don't think much of that at all. I mean, the drawing is all very clever, I'm sure – all the little details and everything – and it does look very like her (I saw her coming out of the ladies, and the resemblance was quite remarkable), but why is it all gold? Why does she have those bands of orange and red all over her? Not my sort of thing at all. But then they say there's three people wanting to buy it already, so there's no accounting for taste, is there? And what brings you here?

~

Sir Gervase told me you were a sure bet, and I've never known him be wrong. He told me I only had to give you a chance, and we'd be laughing. He was damned right. Best night we've had in the gallery for years. People can't get enough of you.

Now, let me introduce you to the de Beauforts – they're very interested in your work. I think they might be after a commission if you play your cards right. Everyone thinks society portraiture was killed off by the camera, but I tell you it ain't so. All the best families want their portraits done, and something like this – the ink drawings with watercolour washes – is different enough to get people talking. You could be the society artist of a generation, Tommy. Think of it!

~

Tommy, dear, isn't this fabulous? Gervase and I are so pleased to finally get you started. When Anabelle said she wanted to marry an artist, we might have had our reservations, but it isn't as though she *needed* a husband to provide for her. Then we saw your art, and we just knew you were special. I'm so proud of you tonight, dear. Really jolly proud.

~

Two words for you: Love. It. Your work has this balance of the high life and real life that is so fresh – very now. Here's my card. Call me in the morning, and we'll see about setting you up for a piece in our Sunday supplement next month.

~

Can't get enough of you, can they, Tommo? Bloody morons. Just overheard somebody telling the idiot who runs this place that they want to buy the triptych you did of the Orient Express crossing that viaduct. I mean, even you know that one's a bit shit, right? God. Didn't imagine this in the old days, did we? Smoking our fags and drinking that piss the King's Head called beer. Those were the days, eh? Before all this hype. Before Anabelle. Still, nice work if you can get it. Don't forget the rest of us when you're famous, will you? Bloody bastard.

~

Daddy says you're a hit, darling. Didn't I say you would be? That one of me collecting the dahlias has just been sold. I told you someone would want it. It seems so fantastic that my face will be on somebody's wall somewhere, doesn't it?

~

When I look at *Anabelle in the Grand Jardin*, I see this Picasso thing going on. Do you know what I mean? Not in terms of colour or shape or medium or anything like that, of course. But in the feel of it – the raw emotion. When you know about art as I do, you get a sense for these things. Your work reminds me of this marvellous artist I saw at the Louvre last year. Do you know the Louvre? Fabulous place – you should go.

~

Bastard. Why you, Tommo? Don't fucking touch me. Bastard.

~

Yes, darling, I think you're right. Time to go home.

Anna, 1984

She will become an expert in this, Rachel supposes – easing each button badge through the thick denim, wiggling it just enough to get free, not so much it leaves a hole. She glances at each one as she tosses it into the pile on Henry's bed: Pac-Man, Wham!, Frankie Say Relax. There is a Rupert Bear one that's maybe meant to be ironic. She's not sure anymore.

Once the last badge is removed, she bundles the dirty vest up with a pair of grey Y-fronts from under Henry's desk. For a moment, her hand hovers over his notebook. She sees him scribbling in it sometimes, eyebrows down, lip bitten. Secret diary, perhaps? Love letters? Angry poems about Margaret Thatcher? Rachel hesitates another second, then turns away. She must become an expert in this too – in the not-knowing. She must learn which questions to ask and when not to speak to his friends, and what time to allow him out to on Saturday night. And she will become an expert in all these things at exactly the same time she has become one in every part of being a mother: just a little too late.

When Henry was a baby, Rachel had worked out the best way to soothe his gums just as his last tooth came through. She became adept at the humdrum small talk of toddler groups, just as he grew old enough for school. She learned the offside rule the week before he switched his allegiance to cricket. She is always becoming the parent her boy needs as her boy becomes somebody new.

Rachel sticks her head into the living room on the way to the washing machine. Henry is home, sitting shoulder to shoulder with Francis on the new sofa.

'How was cricket practice?' she asks.

''K.' Henry's eyes slide away from the end of the six o'clock news. 'When's dinner? I'm starving.'

'Soon. There's half a sandwich left for you in the fridge if you can't wait.'

Henry lopes from the room, and Rachel takes his seat. Francis kisses the side of her head without taking his eyes from Sue Lawley. The And Finallys have started, and a picture of a rocket appears on the screen. Rachel hugs the bundle of laundry to her chest.

'Meant to tell you about this,' Francis says. 'Saw it in the paper on the bus. Thought you might be interested. You've always liked this sort of thing.'

A new photograph fills the screen: a woman in astronaut-blue, stars and stripes on her arm, wide smile under brown bob.

'First mother in space.' Francis shakes his head. 'I mean, good on her – I'm all for feminism and all that – but...' He sucks his teeth. 'Fancy leaving your one-year-old baby to go into space. Can you imagine?'

Rachel imagines. She slides back thirteen years and imagines leaving behind the nappies and tantrums and 'The Wheels on the Bus'. She imagines waving to Henry as she walks out to her spaceship, helmet tucked under her arm. She feels the pang of guilt that comes with the burst of excitement. She tries to imagine what it must be like to be this woman – to be an expert in emergency medicine and x-ray crystallography and the stars. *Twinkle, twinkle little star. How I wonder what you are.*

'No,' she says. 'I can't imagine.'

Henry comes back into the room, sandwich in one hand, milk glass in the other. He nods at the screen. 'Who's that?'

'An astronaut,' Francis says. 'A mother,' says Rachel.

After dinner, after *Bergerac*, after giving him just enough time to finish the homework he'd told her he'd already finished, Rachel knocks on Henry's bedroom door. He's lying on his bed, head bent over *The Long Walk*.

Rachel steps over his discarded Walkman and sits beside him. 'You should probably think about going to bed.' She has become like this lately – offering, suggesting, nudging. Never ordering. She isn't yet sure if this makes her a better parent.

Henry sighs. He sits up and dog-ears the corner of his page. 'OK.'

They sit in silence for a few seconds before Rachel asks, 'Do you wish I'd been an astronaut?'

Henry gives her that look.

She flushes. 'Don't you think that would've been exciting – if your mum had been an astronaut?'

Henry considers this for longer than she expects. 'Maybe.' He drapes an arm round her shoulders. 'Would've been a bit weird though, wouldn't it? Nobody's mum's an astronaut. That's not what mums do.'

Rachel nods. 'You're right. It's not what mums do.'

She pauses at the door. Turns back to her boy. 'Do you want me to tuck you in?'

Henry snorts. 'No thanks. I'm fine.'

On the landing, Rachel presses a hand to her chest, pushing back the cramping loss that is not new to her – that doesn't ease no matter how many times she tells herself she is being ridiculous. She stands a full minute in the dark, allowing Henry to spin a little further from her. She braces herself against the pull and thrust of his life as it gathers momentum, ready to break free from her orbit. And she knows that one day – when it is a little too late – she will become an expert in this too.

Only Asking

'I was only asking,' you say, as if that makes it better – as if she has no right to be offended.

Anabelle looks at you in her dressing table mirror. 'Is that what you think of me?'

'I'm just curious.' You loosen your bowtie, sit on the edge of the bed to untie your laces. 'If marrying me had meant being poor – if your father had threatened to cut you off without a penny, say – would you still have done it?'

'It was 1975, Tommy.' She shakes her head. 'Not 1850. This isn't *The Barchester Chronicles*. There was never any question of me being cut off for marrying you.'

'I know that.' You could drop this now. If you hadn't had that third whisky, you would too. You never argue with Anabelle. 'I'm just saying supposing. If you had no trust fund of your own – if you hadn't been from a Nice Family – would you still have married me?'

She starts pulling the pins from her hair, tossing each one into the jewelled trinket box you bought her last time you were in Paris. 'Do you think coming from a 'nice family' made it easier to marry you?' She meets your eyes in the mirror. 'Because Mother and Daddy might've liked you but the rest of the family, the rest of...' She stops. And you know she was going to say *society* – the rest of *society* didn't think much of you at all, not back then.

'I know how it was.' You lean back on the quilted counterpane. 'Everyone was horrified you picked the unwashed artist.'

Anabelle softens. 'But you won them over, didn't you?' She laughs. 'People invite us out because they want to see you now, not me.'

It's probably true. Now you are officially an up-and-coming artist – albeit one approaching forty – everyone is a lot keener to be photographed with you for *Tatler*. Which is why it's midnight and you have just got in from another dinner sandwiched between Clara, who can never talk of anything but The Children, and Clara's husband, whose only interest is this new FTSE 100 nonsense.

'You haven't answered the question,' you say. 'Because we wouldn't have been a bit poor, Bella. It wouldn't have been a case of not being able to send the girls to Bute House or take a winter break in the Dordogne. It would've been the kind of poor where we might not have eaten some days. We would never have lived anywhere that had heating, let alone turned it on. And it might've been forever. I might never have made any money.'

'Of course you would.' She clicks the silver clasp and slips the box back into its drawer. 'You would've still been the same artist. Still just as talented.'

Would you? Without a father-in-law with the money and connections in the art world to give you your first exhibition, would *society* be queuing at the door to have you draw their portraits? You didn't marry Anabelle for her money, but she brought it with her anyway. She rolls the dice so you land on a ladder every time. And sometimes, when you've had too much to drink, you hate how easy she's made it – how much you feel like a fraud.

'You would've chosen somebody else, wouldn't you?' You pick at the scab again, wanting her to be as uneasy with how easy your marriage has been as you are. 'You wouldn't have looked twice at me – not if a nice banker had come along instead.'

Anabelle pauses, brush halfway to her hair. Your words hang hard and sharp in the soft glow of the bedside lamps. She gets to her feet, and you think she will walk out on you as you deserve. This is the moment the time bomb explodes, and you mess up your outrageous good fortune at last.

She stands beside the bed, looking down at you. 'I would've got a job,' she says in a tight voice. 'I would've learned to type or taken in ironing or something. I would've worked so that you didn't have to give up drawing. Because I love you. I fell in love with your drawings, and then I fell in love with you. That's why I married you.' She sinks down beside you. 'I don't know if I could've been content if we were poor. Is anybody poor content with it? But the answer to your question is yes, I would still have married you.'

Of course she would. You knew that all along.

Anabelle waits until the silence has stretched tight overhead before saying, 'What would you have done?' She looks at you. It's her turn to ask questions – questions she would never have dreamed of asking if you hadn't asked first. 'Would you have kept on drawing if we were starving? Or would you have given it up to support me – to have a family?'

You've said too much to be dishonest now. You shake your head. 'I don't know.'

'What about someone else then?' she says. 'Would you have given up art for somebody else?'

What can you say? Somebody Else didn't give you the chance. Somebody Else sent back your ring in an envelope with a one-line note. Somebody Else is Somewhere Else with Someone Else. Anabelle was the one who said yes – it is Anabelle who has stuck with you for more than a decade. Anabelle and her kind heart and her trust fund.

The silence creeps on until your wife gets to her feet. 'Well,' she says, 'I was only asking.'

Christa, 1986

Here it is again. For maybe the tenth time, the TV screen fills with the same footage. Rachel watches as the shuttle launches, arching its way towards space. She listens to the familiar cheers. She waits without breathing for the terrible flash. And there it is: the flash, the manic contrails parachuting across the clear blue sky. She doesn't realise she's crying until Francis encloses one of her hands in both of his, shuffles an inch closer on the sofa.

In the coming weeks, people will start talking about O-rings and lower than average temperatures at the launch site. News reporters will speculate about all the delays and how many warnings might have gone unheeded. Seven asteroids will be given new names. Today though, people are only talking about her – Christa McAuliffe, the Teacher in Space.

Rachel has read everything about Christa – about this history teacher who was given a seat aboard a rocket. Newspapers and TV chat shows have been full of her. Christa was only one year younger than Rachel. Christa was a wife. Christa had children. Dear God, she had children. Were they there at the launch? Did they see it all happen? Rachel slides her free hand into the hand of her teenage son, and, for once, he doesn't pull away.

They are showing the footage of them walking out to the bus again now. Seven astronauts, smiling in their blue jump-suits: Dick, Judy, Ron, Mike; Christa is fifth in line; behind her, Ellison and Greg wave to the crowd. They are buoyant, excited. They are going to space. Rachel closes her eyes.

Later tonight, President Reagan will tell his grieving nation about the pain of expanding man's horizons. Sombre-faced and black-tied, he will declare that the future is not for the faint-hearted. Rachel, hearing the speech on the radio over breakfast, will cry into her cornflakes because two children had a mum who dared to go to space, and who so very nearly made it, and who won't ever make it back. Christa's President will tell the whole world how daring and brave she was, how she had a hunger to explore the universe and find out its truths. And Rachel will cry for Christa because at least Christa tried.

Dearly Departed

Dublin.

    Madrid.

    Lisbon.

'There it is.' Francis slaps Henry on the back. 'Calgary. Terminal Three.'

Rachel turns her gaze from the departure board to her son. She has had to look up to see into his eyes for three years now, but it still takes her by surprise. She still expects to see a tiny face pressed against her thigh, sticky hands clutching the hem of her blouse.

'Do you want us to come with you to the desk,' she says. 'We've got two hours until our train.'

'No need.' Henry bends to kiss her cheek then pulls a wilting posy from the side pocket of his rucksack. 'Here. I picked these for you this morning. I know you'll say I shouldn't, but...' He shrugs. 'Special occasion.'

Rachel takes the flowers from him: bright white yarrow, garish campion, a solitary star of woody nightshade from the hedge by the front gate. She nods and then turns back to the board until her eyes clear.

    Rome.

    New York.

Henry scans the sign hanging from the strip-lighted ceiling. Gentlemen's Hairdresser and Nursing Mothers to the left. Departures straight ahead.

'Take care of yourself then.' Francis's voice is gruff with suppressed tears. 'See you in a few months.'

Rachel has only seen Francis cry once. On the day Henry was born, he had kissed her sweat-soaked head and cried as he asked her to name their son. Eighteen years later, it seems absurd that she should ever have had to choose. He is Henry. Of course he's Henry. And now Henry is walking away from her, red Kick Hi boots squeaking on the shiny floor, and there is *no need* for her to travel even another few steps with him.

Three flights disappear off the board. Three more take their place.

Tokyo.

Buenos Aires.

Sydney.

A crew of British Airways hostesses clop past, professional smiles fixed above striped dresses. In another few seconds, Henry disappears from sight behind them.

Rachel takes Francis's arm. 'Come on.'

Francis checks his watch. 'We've still got lots of time to kill. Where do you want to go?'

Rachel thinks. Venice, perhaps, or Vienna. The Amazon basin. The markets in Marrakesh. She would like to go to a debutante ball in Edwardian England and a nineteenth-century archaeological dig in the Middle East. She would like to sit in the amphitheatres of ancient Greece and turn to Roald Amundsen at the South Pole and say, *well isn't this quite something?* She would like to visit the galleries of Paris as she had planned to do, half a lifetime ago, with a man who had fitted her perfectly, whom she had loved, whom she had sent away for what must have been a good reason at the time. A man who hadn't come back to try again.

'There's a café where you can see the planes taking off,' Francis says. 'We could go there?'

'Yes.' Rachel nods. 'Lovely.'

At a corner table, with a Chelsea bun and a second-hand copy of *Moon Tiger*, Rachel concentrates on not thinking about Henry. She can feel Francis trying to not think about Henry too. Francis's grief is in letting go – being unable to ask their son to stay with them; Rachel's grief is in being unable to ask their son to take her with him. When she catches Francis's eye over the top of his newspaper, he is looking at her with that familiar bafflement and determination – as if she's a puzzle he has committed his life to solving. She wishes she had a solution to give him.

'Look.' Francis places his newspaper on the salt-scattered Formica. He nods at the window and the Air Canada plane taxiing towards the runway. 'There he goes.'

Rachel smoothes the edge of her paper napkin, replaces a crusted ketchup bottle in its wire basket. She will not get up and press herself to the window. She will not bang on the smeared glass.

'You wish you were going too, don't you?' Francis is watching her. 'You want us to have our own Big Adventure.'

From the way he says the words, she knows he is thinking of jungles and Antarctic treks, eating tarantulas and walking across hot coals on some remote Pacific Island. To Francis, adventure is a place of extremity.

'Because we can, you know.' He smiles a brave smile. 'If that's what you want.'

What Rachel wants most right now is to be content. She wants to not be the kind of wife who insists on standing outside on January nights, trying to spot Orion, or who calls him to paddle in a river when he's wearing his new trousers. This man, who wants nothing more than a fortnight in Brighton every August, deserves contentment.

'I don't know,' she says, even though she does. 'I've not yet been on a plane, so maybe a little trip somewhere would be nice.'

The plane has reached the top of the runway.

'OK.' Francis nods. 'OK, we will.'

She slides her hand across the table to his. 'It doesn't have to be anywhere fancy. A little adventure, not a big one.'

Francis's eyes rest on the nearest departure board.

Los Angeles.

Paris.

Then a sudden smile brings him back to her.

'A cruise,' he says. 'How about an all-inclusive cruise? Stanley took his wife on one last year – absolutely raved about it. Good British food, entertainment in the evenings – we wouldn't even have to get off the ship if we didn't fancy it. Sound good?'

The plane begins to gather speed. Rachel's fingers drift to the window.

'Rachel?'

The wheels leave the tarmac, and something invisible tethering her to the plane snaps. She traces the line of its ascent with her fingers, lifting it with all her strength, sending it soaring out towards the horizon and to whatever lies beyond.

'Yes.' She can't look away. 'A cruise would be lovely.'

All That's Left to Say

I think he has gone. From the way Rachel is looking at him, I know she thinks so too. Her father, my husband – he is gone, and neither of us wants to be the one to say it. We don't want to be the one to call an end – to reach behind Peter's bed for the buzzer to summon a nurse, who will examine him with professional tenderness and then speak the words that will make me a widow. I continue to stroke the back of his hand. It's still warm.

'He loved you, you know.' I look across the cream waffle blanket to where Rachel sits, straight-backed in her plastic chair. 'Daddy loved you so much.'

'I know.' She sounds surprised as if Peter's love is not the love she ever doubted. 'I know he did.'

I lost Peter a year ago. That's what people tell me, anyway, as if he is a displaced ornament or the strength in my back. They tell me I lost him when he stopped remembering who I was – that first Sunday I sat with him in the recreation room, and he told me that I wasn't quite as beautiful as his young wife but very nearly. When I go for coffee with my friends, they tell me that the Peter I married went missing sometime in those deceitful months between Easter (when we laughed together as we found his missing car keys in the fridge) and

Boxing Day (when he was brought home barefoot in his pyjamas by the beat policeman at 3 a.m.). And they are so very wrong. Because until now, I have been able to tell him a joke and watch him laugh, even if he didn't quite get it. Until now, he has squeezed my hand when I've squeezed his. I've been able to listen to the radio with him and knit him socks.

Tomorrow, when I wake, Peter will not be beside me, and it won't be because he is sleeping in his mauve-painted room at Dunbar Lodge. It will be because he is not. He was, and now he is not. I have not been careless enough to lose my husband. I've kept my eyes on him every minute as he has been ripped from me.

'Mamma?' Rachel leans forward, lays a hand on his chest. She hasn't called me Mamma for years. 'I think he's...'

'I know.' I smile at her. 'Let's give ourselves another moment with him, shall we?'

'He was such a good dad.' Rachel squeezes her eyes shut. 'He loved me so much.'

'He did.' I can feel the tears coming. I'm not ready for them. I'm not ready to start the finality of grief. 'He loved being a father.'

'He was the best.'

The best father in the whole world? Or the best parent she had? Both perhaps. And that's what I'd wanted, wasn't it? Their relationship had been my one indulgence as a mother. I'd tried to do everything right: Rachel had slept outside in her pram two hours every day; I'd not cuddled her more than I could help; I'd weaned her on liver and tripe to help her grow. I used to listen to older mothers in the park, and I'd tried to do what they did – to cover my inexpert mothering with pilfered advice. But I'd allowed Peter to spoil her just a little – allowed him not to worry himself too much about discipline. I thought that was what they needed to love each other.

Was it my desperation to witness the love between these two that made my own love so hard to put into words? Somehow those three words that are meant to come naturally – the ones I'd never heard from my own mother – wouldn't come. Sometimes I would want to say them – to spill love at her feet – and somehow, the moment would always pass in platitudes. And so I'd save up £3 so Rachel could get a new party dress, and I'd cut articles from newspapers about women doing amazing things and leave them under her pillow. I made sure she married a man who would care for her. I held her newborn baby for her so she could sleep an hour or two. I found ways to tell her what I couldn't seem to tell her.

'Why didn't you have more?' Rachel says. She gets up and draws the grey polyester curtains against the dusk. 'Why did you only have me?'

I have been waiting for this question for over forty years.

'We couldn't,' I say. 'For medical reasons.'

It's the truth and something a little less than the truth. And I hope delicacy will stop her asking for more. I don't have the strength to unstitch the history Peter and I have created for our daughter. I can't wind it back into a ball now and make it into something of a different pattern. It's too late. We couldn't have more children for medical reasons. That's all she needs to know.

'But we had you.' I look at the framed photo on Peter's bedside table. The three of us with Francis on Rachel's wedding day. 'You were all we needed.'

She comes back to the bed and plants a kiss on Peter's forehead. She brushes away a tear. Her hand hovers at the red button on the wall. 'Shall I?'

I nod. We hear the faint cry of the buzzer from somewhere down the corridor.

'Was I really enough?' Rachel crosses the worn carpet to my side of the bed. 'Was I enough for you?'

'Of course.' I lay Peter's hand down on the blanket. It is beginning to cool. 'Of course you were.'

Footsteps are hurrying down the corridor towards us.

'Rachel, I...' I squeeze her hand, feeling a paralysing weight of urgency. 'I...'

I still can't say it.

'I know, Mamma.' She looks at me with eyes so like her father's. 'I love you too.'

Sketches of a Broken Heart

You stand for a moment in the grey-pink dusk, a stranger outside your own studio. What are you going to say to her? How are you going to say it? Annabelle would be better at this than you. But Bessie hasn't chosen her mother. She hasn't even chosen Lottie. By coming here – to the one place in the world that is yours alone – she has chosen you.

They didn't tell you about this. When you told people that you had twin daughters, nobody said it would be up to you to heal a broken heart – to examine it, turn it gently in your hands and proclaim, *it's OK, I think we can fix it.* You'd imagined bike rides and teaching them to draw. You were ready to buy emergency tampons and learn to French plait. You hadn't thought as far as boyfriends.

Bessie looks up as the door creaks. She is curled in your chair, sleeves of her school jumper pulled down against its cold metal frame. Her bloodshot eyes are rimmed with smudged mascara. She points to the drawing on your ink-flecked desk. 'Who's that?'

You cross to her side. 'A friend of mine.'

'Why have I never met him then?'

'He's dead. Died when you were small.'

'Oh.'

You examine the paper together. The drawing hasn't turned out how you intended. You'd wanted to capture Rupert in his youth – flamboyant, cynical, foolish. But he had come out like this: lined and gaunt, a cigarette at his lips, judging eyes.

'Why is he yellow?' Bessie says. 'You always paint loads of different colours over your drawings. Why's he just yellow?'

'That's how he was last time I saw him.' You look away. 'He'd drunk himself yellow.'

Bessie sniffs and wipes her nose on her sleeve. You take a deep breath. You can't get this wrong; you have no idea how to get it right.

'Lottie said you and Aaron split up.'

She nods. 'He dumped me.'

'Want to talk about it?'

When she doesn't answer, you pull an empty sheet of cartridge paper and one of your best pens across the desk. 'Want to draw about it?'

She doodles at first. As you pull up the spare chair beside her, she creates spirals and hearts pierced with arrows. Then she begins to draw herself, eyes cast down, hair hanging across her face. She's good at this. Lottie is good too but has no interest in art. Lottie wears oversized Alanis Morissette T-shirts and hammers out Pearl Jam riffs on her guitar. It's Bessie who has found her voice in drawing. And so you draw together, side-by-side, self-portraits of a crushed teen and a baffled father.

'Were you ever dumped, Dad?' It's quarter of an hour before Bessie speaks again. 'Before you married Mum, I mean.'

'Yes.'

'Was it shit?'

You don't flinch. You're getting better at this – the not-flinching when you hear them swear, or when you pick them up from house parties at 11 p.m. and watch them push a path to the door through black bottles of K Cider, teenagers pressed close together in corners. You are teaching yourself to be OK.

'Yes,' you say. 'Really shit.'

'Did you... did you love her?'

You try not to think about it. 'I suppose so.'

'So why didn't it work out?'

'Lots of reasons. We were young.'

And you realise with a curious horror that she had been Bessie's age. You were nineteen, and the girl you loved – the girl you thought you'd marry – was the same age your daughters are now. For a few seconds, the impossibility of it stills your hand. What if Bessie had been waiting in here for a different reason today? What if, instead of dumping her, Aaron had bought her a ring from a market stall? Bessie and Lottie are still children. They still dance in their pyjamas to the Spice Girls and insist on stockings at Christmas. It wasn't like that with you and her. You must've been more grown-up somehow.

'Aaron said he loved me.' Bessie adds a single melodramatic tear to the cheek of her portrait. 'But I don't think he really did. If people love you, they don't dump you, do they?'

Three decades on, and that question still pinches at you, still settles itself deep in your gut. If somebody loves you, they don't leave you. They don't send back your ring. They don't give up on you. Do they?

'First love is too powerful for some people,' you say. 'But you can survive it. I promise.'

Bessie puts her pen aside and picks up the drawing of Rupert. 'Why did you draw him? You draw people who pay you to draw them, or you draw me and Lottie and Mum. You don't draw dead people.'

'I suppose it's a different kind of love. He was an idiot, but he was funny and generous and fierce.' You smile at Rupert. 'Maybe I draw the things I don't want to forget.'

Bessie unfolds herself from the chair. 'Well, it's the best picture you've ever done.' She says it with a seventeen-year-old's certainty, no room for argument. 'You'll probably get like a million pounds for it, or something.'

She leans over and wraps her arms around your shoulders. 'Thanks, Dad.'

You don't know what you've done.

At the door, she pauses. 'You shouldn't leave him all yellow like that.' She shrugs. 'If you loved him, then he wasn't only yellow to you, was he?'

And suddenly, you are not so sure that Bessie is still a child. She is both more and less: a twilight creature caught between the glare of adulthood and the strange, bright magic of before. And you hope she stays there for a while, just a little longer, just long enough for you to capture it in pen and ink.

For a few minutes after she has gone, you continue to look at Rupert's face. Then you pick up your brush, and you start to paint.

Whodunit

It's during the final ad-break of *Midsomer Murders* that Francis asks Rachel if she thinks they have a good marriage. She knows he has been thinking about it ever since Henry's wedding when the vicar said that the biggest threat to marriage was complacency. *Don't think you have a good marriage,* he said. *If you think you have a good marriage, then you won't work at it.* She could see Francis frowning in the pew next to her, shaking his head vigorously enough that she had to nudge him in case Laura's parents saw. Henry had made it clear from the first time he brought Laura to Sunday lunch that she was The One and that Rachel and Francis were to do everything to impress her and her family or, at the very least, not embarrass him.

'*Do* you think it's good?' Francis says, turning down the volume on the man telling them about *vorsprung durch technik*.

'Do you?' Rachel says.

'Of course, but do you?'

'If I say yes, does that mean our marriage is in trouble?' She laughs. Francis doesn't. And she thinks she should say something different, something more, but the advert has finished, and Francis turns up the sound, and they wait for John Nettles to tell them who's to blame.

With Fond Regards

You can't quite get her eyes right. It's weird because you've drawn those eyes dozens of times over the last quarter of a century. This always happens on your preliminary sketches – you can't quite capture her – but never on the final drawing like this. In the end, your pictures are always perfectly Anabelle.

Perhaps you are putting too much pressure on yourself. You know that on the morning of your silver wedding anniversary, Anabelle will present you with a thoughtful, discrete gift and a card written on both sides with all her feelings for you. You can't do that. You've never known how to do that. Everything you want to say has to be in this drawing. When she unwraps it and sees herself, she needs to see all the things you don't quite know how to say. What do you say after twenty-five years of marriage anyway?

You could try thank you. You could thank her for marrying you when friends told her you were only after her money. Thank her for not listening to them, or at least not believing them, or at least not believing them enough to say it out loud. Thank her for letting you draw her. Thank her for being the first to speak when Lottie brought a girlfriend home with her at the end of her first term at university – for saying *nice to meet you* and flicking the switch on the kettle, not blurting out some well-meaning idiocy. Thank her for having the right words every time you've been dumb.

You could say sorry too. Sorry that after so many portraits of her, this is the first you've done *for* her. Sorry for the twenty-four anniversary cards that said only *To Anabelle, Love Tommy*. Sorry that Bessie was always a daddy's girl even though you are not the one who went to every school play, every doctor's appointment and piano exam. Sorry that after so many Christmases with her family, you still forget and serve red wine in the white wine glasses.

When you return to her portrait, you can see now what's wrong. How is it that you didn't notice before? You have missed the years out of her eyes. You have drawn her in the centre of her queendom – elegant and laughing in front of her Mason Cash mixing bowl, silver measuring spoons in hand. But you've given her the eyes of a teenage girl, not a woman approaching fifty. You have missed the fine lines, the story-telling creases. And when you try again – when you change this one detail – the picture is completely new. You haven't caught one instant of laughter – you've captured two decades of worrying over school reports, laughing over Sunday after-noon *Dad's Army* repeats, long evenings squinting as she stitched tiny name labels into gym skirts and blazers. Your pen has recorded everything she has poured into the weeks and years of your life. It has not gone unseen. You have seen it. And here it is.

Enough

Rachel can't tell Laura the truth. Now isn't a moment for anything so sharp, so hard-edged as truth. If she tells her daughter-in-law the truth, she would have to tell her this: No.

No (she would have to say), you do not have enough love for this. No, you will not be enough. You will try so hard every day – most days, at least – to be enough of everything your tiny daughter needs, but no, you won't quite make it. She would have to tell her the secret held by each generation of mothers from the next: there will be no hallelujah moment when you realise that you did it! You were enough! You were a good mother! There will only be, if you're lucky, a moment when you realise that you never stood a chance: that your love couldn't contain your child, because children weren't made to be contained; that if you had been everything your child needed, they wouldn't have outgrown you, and if they don't outgrow you then you have failed. There will be a moment when you look at them and realise that they are OK, and you are OK, and they didn't need you to be perfect after all. They only needed you to wish you were.

Rachel can't tell her that now.

So instead, as Laura uncurls from the sofa to hand over Rachel's granddaughter and Rachel feels a rush of love so dizzying she has to sit down, as Laura watches them with jealous, exhausted eyes and asks the question in a cracked, dull voice, Rachel says, 'Don't be silly, Laura. Of course you will. You're going to be a brilliant mother.'

Final Resting Place

The boy springs to his feet as you enter, sending his wooden stool clattering back against the wall. You think *boy*, but he is just about a man – an art student, probably. On the pinboard behind him, there is a print of Anabelle, one of your earliest portraits of her. Next to that, you can see your name at the top of a mauve piece of paper, followed by a few paragraphs of text you can't see clearly but which you are almost sure is a print-out of your Wikipedia page.

It has been thirty years since you were last here. It's less dingy than you remember: there are bigger spaces between the frames on the wall; the card beside each one is typed now; the prices in the bottom corners are much more interesting.

'Can I help?' The boy traces the line of your gaze to Anabelle's face. 'That's by Tommy Granger,' he says. 'Used to exhibit here when he was fresh out of art school – before he was famous, of course.'

Of course. You wouldn't exhibit here now. Not the Great Tommy Granger. That's the implication, and it hits you a little below the ribs. You should've come back. When people started paying you to draw, you should've made the effort to exhibit here again – helped the gallery out. This was, after all, where it all started. If you hadn't been exhibiting that day in 1973 – if you hadn't met Anabelle...

'Between you and me, I'm not the biggest Granger fan.' The boy gives you a conspiratorial grin. 'He's basically a posh Quentin Blake, isn't he?'

'I think that's a bit unfair on Quentin Blake.' You laugh. 'But for my part, I'm deeply flattered by the comparison.'

'You're flattered by...?' The boy frowns, and then his eyes widen. 'Shit. You mean...? You're not...?'

'Tommy Granger. Pleasure to meet you.'

'Oh my God.' He snatches at your offered hand. 'I'm so sorry. I can't believe I just said that.'

'Don't worry about it.' You extract yourself from his grip. 'It's refreshing to hear an honest appraisal.'

Coming back here had been a whim at the end of one of those weeks when galleries and collectors fill your inbox and answering machine every time it clears. One of the few weeks you wished you'd employed an agent. They all want The Picture. Now the portrait that finally won you the National Portrait Award has finished its three-year stint on show, the fight is on to be the one to own it. And you have a feeling that at least half of the people desperate to have it are more attracted by your signature than the inks and water-colours. You'll never get used to that.

'Why don't you show me what you prefer,' you say to the boy. 'If I'm not your cup of tea, show me something here that is.'

The boy's colour deepens. 'I've got a bit of a weird taste.'

You like this boy. He reminds you of you: that gangling awkwardness, that laugh like a tic, that attempt at a worldly shrug, self-consciously aborted in the middle. You were this boy once.

'Have you? Excellent.'

He hesitates, then shrugs. 'What I like best is to go through the old boxes of pictures that were exhibited here but never sold or claimed by the artist. They never throw any of them away. The guy who owns this place said I could keep whatever I wanted.'

'Show me.'

He leads you into the small backroom. From under the desk, he pulls a cardboard box.

'These are my favourites.'

A watercolour of the ocean, in pinks and golds, as if the sun is setting even though it is still high in the purple sky above. A tiny oil of a girl staring straight out of the canvas from behind dirty, tangled hair. A young man, cigarette between his lips, laughing in his ink-spattered shirt as he lolls back on a pub stool. Your breath snags in your throat.

'It's me.'

The boy looks at the last picture in your hand. 'You did that?' he says. 'Really?'

'No.' You shake your head. 'It's *me*. The man in the picture.'

He peers at the laughing man and then at your face, taking away the thirty years between the two. 'Oh my God.'

'My friend Rupert painted it.'

'Rupert?' The boy is staring at you again. 'Like *the* Rupert. The one in your picture?'

'Yes.'

'Wicked.' He leans forward to take another look. 'I think it's brilliant. A bit slapdash maybe, but the way his face – *your* face – is lit, is genius.'

You nod. And you suddenly want to cry. That's exactly what Rupert was: a slapdash genius. This boy can see it, and you want to cry because it is twenty-five years too late to be seen.

'May I have it.' You clutch the painting to your chest. 'I'll swap it with you. You give me Rupert's portrait of me. I'll give you my portrait of Rupert.'

Yes. Perfect. You think of the messages waiting for you at home, the silly numbers being thrown about by dealers who want one up on their rivals.

'I couldn't.' The boy looks horrified. 'It must be worth a fortune. You can have the painting for nothing.'

'No.' It has to be this way. 'If you don't like my drawings, then sell it. Start your own gallery – do whatever you like.'

He tries to protest again, but you stop him. You can't believe you haven't thought of doing something like this before. All the people with the money and the power and the opinions that were never in Rupert's favour shan't own him after all. Rupert always stuck two fingers up at the art world and died furious that nobody saw it or cared.

'Please,' you say. 'It would make me very happy.'

Now they would care. Now, at last, Rupert would win.

Eileen, 2005

On Monday, Sophie is going to be a doctor.

'Come here, Grandma.' She pats the sofa. 'Let me listen to your heart.' She pushes the stethoscope into Rachel's tummy and frowns. 'Very bad,' she says. 'You're very poorly.' She looks at Jake, chewing on a Duplo brick at her feet. 'Jakey's very poorly too.'

She rifles through her first-aid kit: plastic spoons and tiny rolls of bandage. 'Were you ever a doctor, Grandma?'

Rachel thinks of all the nights she sat by Henry's bedside, holding an old jug while he vomited or stroking his hair as he wheezed himself to sleep. She thinks of plasters and banana medicine, an old tea towel stemming the flow of a ruptured eardrum.

'No,' she says. 'You have to be very clever to be a doctor.'

Sophie snaps the case shut again. 'Good job I'm here then. I can mend a broken heart easy-peasy.'

On Tuesday, Sophie has decided on being a horse rider.

'Megan-in-my-class is having a pony party when she's six,' she says, sitting astride the back of an armchair. 'Did you ever ride a pony?'

Rachel shakes her head. 'Never.' She scrapes soggy cracker crumbs from Jake's tractor jumper. 'You have to be very strong to be a horse rider.'

'I'm strong,' says Sophie. 'Nearly as strong as Megan.'

'I'm going to be a gymnast,' Sophie says as soon as Rachel opens the door on Wednesday morning. 'Megan's going to be one too. She can already do a backflip because she goes to gymnastics on Mondays *and* Thursdays, but Mummy says I can't go.'

Laura rolls her eyes at Rachel and pushes Jake's buggy through the door. 'I said you couldn't go *this week*,' she says. 'Maybe after the holidays.' She turns to Rachel. 'I may be a bit late tonight – meeting at four thirty. Bound to run over.'

Rachel unclips Jake from the buggy and carries him into the kitchen.

'Can you do a cartwheel, Grandma?' Sophie asks. 'I almost can.'

'Not now.' Rachel laughs. 'I used to be able to when I was a little girl.'

'Why can't you now then?'

Rachel hesitates. 'There must have been a point when I stopped turning cartwheels,' she says. 'Eventually, I suppose I forgot I ever could.'

On Thursday, Sophie still wants to be a gymnast.

She crouches on the floor of the living room. 'Look at this, Grandma!' She pushes herself over into a roly-poly, toppling sideways but still leaping to her feet, arms raised. 'Ta-da!'

Rachel claps, and Jake joins in.

At teatime, Sophie frowns at Rachel across the table. 'What *were* you, Grandma?'

'I beg your pardon.'

'Before you were my grandma, what were you? Did you work in a boring bank like Grandpa?'

'Well...' Rachel puts down her fork. 'I worked in the office of a big shop for a few years. I typed letters and sorted out bills and things like that. But then Daddy grew in my tummy, and I spent quite a lot of years looking after him.' For some reason, she is unable to meet Sophie's eyes. 'I did other things too, like... well... I helped with the library and at mother-and-baby clinics. Voluntary things. I still do some of them.'

'Didn't you want to do anything else? Like be an explorer or a gymnast?'

Rachel smiles. 'An explorer would've been fun, but people thought women shouldn't do things like that back then. There were only a few jobs we could do.' She thinks about it. She thinks of her school friends, emerging from the sixties as nurses and secretaries and housewives, but also as doctors and lecturers. 'At least, that's what I thought,' she says. 'That's what I was told.'

'That's stupid.' Sophie stabs a fish finger. 'Daddy says I could be an explorer. He says I'm brave enough to do anything.'

'I'm sure he's right.'

'He said he'd like to be an explorer too, and Mummy said that would suit him because he'd be able to leave all his reponsobilities behind.' She slurps her squash. 'What are reponsobilities? Why can't you take them with you when you go exploring?'

On Friday, Sophie is crying.

'Argument with Megan,' Laura whispers not quietly enough. 'Good luck.'

'She said I can't be a gymnast.' Sophie kicks off her sandals and follows Rachel and Jake into the kitchen. 'She said you have to be able to do a backflip to be a gymnast.'

'So what?' Rachel opens the biscuit tin. 'You could learn to do a backflip if you wanted, and much better things besides.'

Sophie sniffs and takes a custard cream. 'What's better than doing a backflip?'

Rachel considers the question. 'How about doing a backflip in a spaceship?'

'Nobody can do that, Grandma.'

'One woman already has, just last week. The first person ever.'

And so she shows Sophie. She sits at her computer with Sophie on her lap, and they watch the video clip Henry sent her. They watch the space shuttle turn a slow 360-degree flip, nose-to-tail, clouds scudding beneath it across the Earth's atmosphere.

'They do it to check for damage,' Rachel says. 'One astronaut does the backflip, and other astronauts in the space station above take photos of the spaceship.'

'Do you have to be clever to be an astronaut?' Sophie doesn't take her eyes from the screen.

'Very clever.'

'And brave?'

'Oh yes.'

'And strong?'

'Definitely strong.'

'That's what I'm going to be then.' Sophie nods and slips from Rachel's lap. 'I'll be an astronaut and do backflips in my spaceship.'

On Saturday evening, Rachel finds an e-mail from Henry in her inbox.

I take it this is your doing? ;)

She clicks on the attached photo, and her screen fills with her granddaughter. Sophie is dressed in a sequined leotard, standing in a cardboard box with portholes drawn on the side. She has a foil-covered shoebox as a jet pack and a metal colander on her head. The expression on her face is fierce. Rachel looks at her for a full five minutes before replying.

I hope so. I really hope so.

Review: *Images of a Lost Youth* by Tommy Granger ★★★☆☆

What do you think of when you think of Tommy Granger? Whatever it is, it's almost certainly not what you find at the latest Bankside exhibition. Yes, here is a collection of exquisitely detailed ink drawings, washed over and highlighted in bold watercolours. Look closer, however, and you'll see that this is not your usual Granger. Instead of uncompromising portraits of London high society, and the more intimate portrayals of his family, this latest collection brings something new. It is not necessarily something better.

There are no portraits in this exhibition. Instead, we are faced with a series of still-lives – scenes, as the title suggests, from Granger's youth. Or so he says. His choice of subjects is curiously lifeless: an open tin of peaches, a football pools coupon next to a Bush wireless, a brown school satchel abandoned beside a bus stop. They are interesting snatches of social history perhaps but lack something of the life and movement of Granger's usual work. The colours, on the whole, are more muted, the brushwork more timid. Compare *Mam*, with its shades of taupe and brown, its tiny undefined figure in one corner with her back turned, with Granger's 1981 piece *Mother* – an intensely evocative portrait of his wife with their newborn twins, wide stripes of soft greens and dusty blues suffusing the work with tranquillity.

There can be no doubt that Granger did indeed come from humble beginnings. There can also be no doubt that much of what is on display here is as technically brilliant as his previous work. There is, however, a lack of authenticity about it. The mawkish memories of a 1950s working-class childhood don't quite ring true from the pen of a man who has spent the last twenty years earning his living from drawing landed gentry. Let's not forget that Granger's most notable work in recent years, the award-winning *Rupert at the End*, is widely believed to be a portrait of his close friend, Harrow-educated Rupert Wingfield-Scott. Granger is also, of course, married to the elder daughter of renowned critic and collector Sir Gervase Crompton.

Among the drawings of empty pint glasses and burned-down cigarettes, there is one stand-out piece that rescues this exhibition from the realms of best-forgotten. *Empty Swings* is reminiscent of Granger's finer work. On the surface, it is merely a pair of swings common in all playgrounds of the 1960s, but there is a hint of movement. The swings are not hanging still. They are twisting away from each other as if a pair of children have just leapt from them to a place only just beyond the gaze of the viewer. An ode to the loss of innocence perhaps, or a suggestion of life's forward momentum, continually moving children towards adulthood. As in *Rupert at the End*, there is one predominant background colour – pink this time – with the same addition of flecks and tendrils of gold.

The last picture in the collection is *Ritz Paris from the Outside*. The incongruity of such a glamorous setting is all the more stark when you realise that this isn't a drawing of the Ritz Paris. Rather, it is of the Palais Garnier as viewed from an upper window *inside* that famous hotel. So who is outside? Is it us, the viewers? Or does this symbolise for Granger the moment when he finally lost his youth and stepped from working-class Britain to high-class Paris, finding himself an outsider in both?

This is not the exhibition that is going to make Tommy Granger's name immortal. If you enjoy his style of art, then it is well worth a visit, but don't expect to find much more than technical mastery and pop social history here. The story he is telling doesn't feel complete. This story isn't quite real.

Vocabulary Test

Rachel finds him at dawn, three branches up the ancient hornbeam. As she walks across the dew-soaked grass towards him, Henry swipes at his eyes with the sleeve of his suit jacket.

'Room for one more?' Rachel gets hold of the bottom branch, braces one foot on the trunk.

'Careful, Mum.' Henry leans down towards her. 'You're not as young as you were.'

'Oh, piffle.' Rachel heaves herself up. It takes three attempts. 'Nor are you, and you're up here.'

They sit in silence for a moment as Rachel gets her breath back. She isn't sure what she is going to say. In forty-two years of parenthood, she has done so many firsts: first words, steps and days at school; first girlfriend and first time behind the wheel of a car; first job, first house. There is a vocabulary of beginnings – squeals of delight, lavish praise, words of proud caution. She doesn't know how to deal with ends. It's a language she hasn't yet learned.

'You'll ruin that suit,' she says, brushing a tuft of moss from his pinstriped leg.

Henry shrugs. 'I called in sick. Couldn't face it today. Don't know what to say to everyone.'

Rachel nods and picks at the bark. There are so many words she will have to unlearn. And she worries that she'll get it wrong somehow. She will find her tongue betraying her with words that don't belong together anymore. *Daughter-in-law. My son's wife. Laura and Henry.* Even though she saw it coming – has been expecting it for over a year, ever since they announced they were pregnant again, ten years after Jake – it is still raw, still fills her with desperate, helpless grief for her son.

'Olivia didn't save us,' Henry says. 'She didn't save our marriage.'

'Babies never do.'

'I don't understand.' Henry looks down at Rachel with an expression that hurts something deep inside her. 'We were in love. Madly in love. You saw us when we married, Mum. We were in love, weren't we?'

'You were.'

'Then what happened?' He rubs at his eyes again. 'I don't know when that stopped. I didn't even know it had stopped until...' He bites his lip.

Rachel searches for the words. She can't find them among the new ones that have crept into their conversations over the last six months: *decree nisi, joint custody*, and the words of the day – *decree absolute*.

'I suppose,' she says, 'you grew up differently.'

'But we were already adults when we met. We knew everything about each other before we married. And yet she's telling me I'm not the man she married anymore.'

'Of course you're not.' Rachel reaches up and places a hand on his knee. 'You don't stop growing up. Not at eighteen or twenty-five or when you marry. Marriage can't be a commitment to stay the same person you were on your wedding day.

That would be absurd. It can only ever be a commitment to change together.'

Henry turns his head away. 'I wish we'd known that fifteen years ago.'

There is a movement on the other side of the garden. Francis has appeared through the French windows, still in his brown-checkered dressing gown. He walks towards them across the lawn. When he reaches them, he looks up at Henry. For a few seconds, their eyes meet, and then Francis kicks off his soaked slippers and begins to climb.

'Jesus, Dad. What are you doing?'

Francis slips, and for a second, Rachel thinks he will fall, but with a grunt, he is up, clinging to a branch by Henry's ankles. Rachel has never seen Francis climb a tree before. He steadies himself before hauling up one more branch so his head is level with Henry's shoulder.

'I'm being here,' he says. 'I'm just... being here.'

And so they sit. For a while, Rachel tries to think of more words of comfort, better advice. Then she stops trying. She sits in the tree with her wordless husband and silent son and the pain they can't share equally. There will be plenty of time for choosing careful words over the next few months. Rachel will probably choose the wrong words too often. Maybe, if she's lucky, she will pick the right ones too. But for now, they sit and watch the sun creep over the laurel hedge, and they don't say anything at all.

Peggy, 2017

High above their heads – above the blossom-heavy hawthorn branches, above the single cloud, eerie in the moonlight – there is a woman. She is a woman who has been labelled with many superlatives. She has been the First. She has done the Most. And now, at fifty-seven, she is the Oldest.

Rachel wonders whether she herself is old. Is this the year when she will officially become old? Magazines tell her that seventy is only the beginning – it's the new forty, or maybe fifty, but not old, no definitely not old. Rachel isn't so sure. People have started giving up their seats for her on the bus. When she took her laptop in to be fixed, the woman at the counter spoke very slowly and loudly, pausing every few words in case Rachel needed to catch up.

Sophie doesn't think of her as old. She has told Rachel as much. But then, Sophie thinks anything less than four and a half billion years old is quite new. As they sit together on the hilltop, high above the haze of a thousand lampposts, Rachel watches her eldest granddaughter as Sophie watches the sky. Sophie is only sixteen months and four A-levels away from studying the sky at Cambridge – a path she's been planning for herself since she was five.

'Did you know that there are more trees on Earth than there are stars in the galaxy?' Sophie says. 'Loads more.' She looks at Rachel. 'Imagine it, Grandma. There are like three trillion trees on Earth and only a couple of hundred billion stars in the Milky Way.'

'Only.'

Sophie laughs and looks out into the black sky. 'Look.' She points to a bright star in the south. 'See that sort of reddish star? That's Mars.'

Mars. Rachel had known you could see Mars – Venus too, and Jupiter and Saturn. But she'd never known how to work out where they were. Sophie has an app on her phone. She points it at the sky, and it tells you what everything is. It's magical. And sometimes, it ruins the magic.

'Did you know that the biggest mountain on Mars is so wide that if you stood on top, you wouldn't know you were on a mountain?' Sophie plucks another Haribo from the packet between them on the bench. 'The slope would be obscured by the curvature of the planet itself.' She shakes her head. 'Mental.'

Rachel pops a gummy cola bottle in her mouth and stares at Mars.

'Grandma,' Sophie says, 'did you know...'

Rachel smiles to herself in the dark. Sophie's catchphrase has been the same ever since her first term at school. *Did you know that curly c and kicking k make the same sound?* Now, Rachel rarely knows the things Sophie knows. At seventeen, Sophie knows about quantum mechanics and how to put on liquid eyeliner. She has perfected the exasperated eye roll when Henry asks her what time she'll be back from Lydia's, and she can explain the wave-particle duality of light. Sophie is ready to be the First and the Most and the Youngest in something, and while Rachel can't wait to see what that something is, she also feels a fear, a creeping unease about all the things Sophie might not yet know.

Did you know that taking no shit from anyone *won't mean anything when Anyone is a man with the keys to your career?*

Did you know that in a thousand insidious ways, you must still be Suitable, even now. There is still a suitable length for your skirt and a suitable volume to speak at and a suitable way to re-spond to a man who is only having a laugh, Love, what's your problem?

Did you know that if you drink too much, or walk home alone, or smile at a stranger, then it is all your fault?

But she probably does know all this. Sophie and her friends who sit round Rachel's table on Thursdays after school, eating biscuits and playing with Snapchat filters, have already seen more of what the world is like than Rachel had at twice their age. They are ready – brilliantly, beautifully, terrifyingly ready – to be Unsuitable Women.

'Did you know,' Rachel says, slipping an arm round Sophie's shoulders, 'there's a woman up there right now, who was the first woman ever to command the ISS? She's done more spacewalks than any other woman on this planet, and she's lived in space for a total of nearly two years.'

Sophie frowns, then nods. 'Yeah. I saw that on the news. She's the old one, right?'

Rachel sighs. 'Yes. And she's the oldest woman ever to go to space. Yes. That too.'

Sophie checks the clock on her phone and groans. 'I've got like a tonne of integration to do for double-maths tomorrow. Dad said he'd pick me up straight from Olivia's ballet lesson so I could get back a bit earlier.'

They wander down the dark path together, back through the gate that leads from the park onto Rachel's street.

'It's cool though, isn't it?' Sophie says. 'The tree thing.' She gestures up at the stars, obscured now by a cloud of orange light. 'It's kinda cool that sometimes you don't have to go on a big adventure to outer space to find amazing stuff.' She pats the grey-green bark of a London plane as they pass. 'Sometimes it's right here.'

Rachel looks at the woman, walking by her side. She thinks of the woman, 40 years older and 250 miles higher. 'Yes,' she says. 'It's pretty cool.'

Rachel

She has already seen you. By the time you spot her, motionless in the doorway of the bar, she is watching you, one hand gripping the frame, the other holding a paperback. For a second, her eyes flick to the French windows that lead onto the hotel terrace, as if she's wondering whether to escape. Perhaps fifty-two years apart is too long for a reunion. Maybe it's not long enough.

She doesn't move. So you push your whisky glass away and get to your feet and say the name you don't ever say. You say it loud enough that the other people at the bar glance over, then follow the line of your gaze. She flushes and hurries across the room.

'Hello,' you say.

'Hello.'

'It's you.'

'Yes,' she says. 'And it's you.'

'Yes.'

You want to touch her. A hug, a kiss, a handshake even. But you don't know how; your hands feel idle and clumsy at your side. You gesture at the array of bottles behind the bar. 'Would you like…?'

Then there you are, on velvet padded stools, two glasses of house white in front of you. Together.

'I suppose you're the artist exhibiting next door,' she says. 'I never thought... It never occurred to me that...' She fiddles with the stem of her glass. 'We're down for the weekend. There's a vintage car rally that Francis wanted to go to.'

Francis. You hadn't known his name before. Her husband – the man she married instead of you – is called Francis. She is Mrs Francis Somebody-or-Other.

'Is Anabelle here?' She takes a sip of her wine. 'Does she come to your exhibitions?'

Even though it is your drawings that have made your wife famous, it's strange to hear Anabelle's name dropping from her lips. It pulls at you, brings you back to the world as it is. And you are able to say that no, Anabelle isn't here this time, although she does often come. And you are able to ask after her health and where she is living now and is she enjoying the sunshine after all that rain. And she says that she is fine and how are you and she doesn't mind the rain because it's good for her garden though sun is always nice. You didn't know she liked to garden.

You drink your wine too fast and are embarrassed until you see her empty glass beside your own. She catches you looking and laughs.

'Do you remember the awful wine we used to drink at Stanley Rec?'

You can remember, but not in the academic way you have remembered for the last five decades. You can taste it, sour and tepid; you can feel the sticky rim of the bottle on your lips as it passes from her to you. If you were foolish enough to let yourself, you'd be able to see it all too. You'd see her huddled beside you on a bench damp with melted frost, fiddling with the pawnshop ring on her left hand.

'They were good times,' you say. The words are meant to be safe and banal. They come out wistful, honest.

You watch her as she plays with the line of beer mats: Jail Ale, Tribute, Fosters. She is not beautiful. Not in the way Anabelle is beautiful. But she is mesmerising in the way she was at seventeen; in the same way you've tried not to draw every time you've picked up your pen for half a century.

'I need some fresh air,' she says, and you think it is a dismissal. But when she stands, she waits for you to stand too.

On the terrace, you try to find something more to say, but you feel no need to fill her in on the half-century she's missed. You don't want to know where she's been and what she's done. Now this moment is here, you don't even want to ask her why she sent back your ring, why she stopped answering your letters. And so you say the only thing you can say.

'I still miss you.'

She glances sideways at you as you walk towards the steps down to the Knot Garden. For a second, she looks confused and then gives that sudden laugh that maybe you had forgotten after all.

'Yes, I miss you too sometimes,' she says. 'Silly, isn't it?'

'I mean... I love Anabelle.'

'Oh yes – Francis is wonderful.'

'But...' You shrug. 'It's you.'

It's her. It has always and never been her. Your life without her has been success and wealth, second homes in London and the Loire Valley, influential in-laws who love you, comfort and ease. Your life with her would've been – what? A fantasy with undefined edges and unknown colour. One you should've forgotten decades ago and never quite could.

'I didn't go to Paris.' She stops at the top of the steps. 'You never took me. So I never went.'

'I'll take you now,' you say. 'Tomorrow. Today.'

She laughs. 'Can you imagine?'

So you imagine. Standing on the terrace together, not touching – still not touching – you imagine. You remember what you had and imagine what still might be. You talk in low voices, and every now and then, one of you laughs so that you can pretend it is only a joke.

'Mrs Flynn?'

You do not notice the concierge until he stops a few feet away.

'Yes?' She turns as if the name belongs to her.

'I managed to book a table at Summerton's,' he says. 'Your husband has returned, so I took the liberty of ordering you a taxi as well.'

'My husband? Oh. Yes, of course.' She smiles. 'Thank you.'

She watches him walk away. 'I have to go.'

She has to go. What else did you expect?

'Lovely to see you again, Tommy.' She touches your arm. 'Or should I be calling you Sir Thomas Granger, now?'

'I'll always be Tommy for you.' You can't look at her as she turns away. 'Lovely to see you too, Mrs Flynn.'

Three Days in the Life Of

Tomorrow she will cry about this. With the bathroom door locked and the shower running hot, Rachel will give herself two minutes – no more – to cry for the What Ifs she left behind five decades ago.

Today, Rachel is having breakfast early. As soon as the restaurant opens, she hurries downstairs, leaving Francis sleeping. If she goes early, she might get in and out before Tommy wakes up. She might not see him. She puts on her lipstick anyway.

At first, she thinks her plan has worked, and she tells herself that she's not disappointed by this. She doesn't see him until his hands appear next to hers at the buffet. And despite the fifty-two years since she last held them, they cannot be any hands but his: a spattering of freckles, the mole on his little finger, the wedding ring.

'Good morning,' he says, and it sounds like an apology.

'Hello.'

Tommy scoops scrambled eggs onto his plate. Rachel dollops yoghurt into her glass bowl. She thinks of all the things she could say. None of them seem possible.

It's Tommy who breaks first. 'Yesterday,' he says and then stops.

'Yesterday.' Rachel looks at him. 'Yes.'

He pulls two rashers of bacon from the hotplate. 'It was... it was...'

'A moment of madness,' she says when he doesn't. 'Behaving like a couple of teenagers at our time of life.'

He replaces the tongs. 'Completely ridiculous.'

'Ludicrous.'

'I love my wife.'

'And I love my husband.'

'She's a good woman.'

'He's a wonderful man.'

'Well then...'

'Well then.'

Yesterday, nothing happened.

Yesterday, Rachel had meant to walk out of the hotel bar. If he hadn't seen her, she might've slipped out by the patio door. If he hadn't said her name, she might've been OK. She might've been able to leave.

Yesterday they had talked, that was all. While Francis was at the rally looking at Sunbeams and Austin 7s, they'd each had one glass of house white. Nothing fancy. They'd reminisced about the last wine they'd drunk together, holding hands on the swings at Stanley Rec. And when they'd reached for their glasses on the bar, their fingertips hadn't quite brushed.

Yesterday they'd walked on the terrace, nothing more. They'd remembered that first kiss in the alley behind the bingo hall. They had dreamed – for half an hour only – of what it would've been like to run away together; of what it would be like to run away together now.

Yesterday they didn't talk of anything in between. Nothing from the Then when he'd given her the ring, to the Now, more than five decades since she sent it back. Perhaps they should have. Maybe they should have talked about Everything After Then. Rachel should've asked Tommy why he didn't fight for her. When her parents told them they had to wait, why didn't he write? Why didn't he wait? Why was she so easy to give up?

Yesterday they didn't hold hands.

They didn't kiss.

They did not run away together.

Today they have fixed their defences.

'It was nothing,' Tommy says. 'One silly conversation. We should forget about it.' He looks at her. 'Shouldn't we?'

Rachel doesn't meet his eye. 'Of course.' She watches the plum-red spatters of compote dripping onto her yoghurt. 'What conversation?'

He nods. 'Exactly. What conversation? What engagement?' He shakes a bottle of ketchup over his plate. 'Ancient history.'

Rachel picks up her glass of orange juice and turns to go, only to find his hand on her wrist.

'Can I ask you one thing, though?' He hesitates. 'Back then... why did you stop answering my letters? Why didn't you just tell me?'

Rachel feels the ground drop away from her. 'What letters?'

He watches her face for a long moment. Then he slides his fingers from her wrist. 'You're right.' He straightens up. 'Of course. What letters?'

And he waits for her to take a table by the window before choosing a table by the door.

Tomorrow, as Rachel rubs shampoo into her grey-streaked hair, she will scold herself again. She will tell herself once more that it is absurd – *she* is absurd. They wouldn't have been happy. She would've resented his ink bottles scattered about their home, or he would've been irritated by how weakly she makes tea or how often she burns toast. They wouldn't have had the life they thought they'd have. They'd been teenagers – too young to understand how love has to survive the mundane far more often than the extraordinary. She will tell herself all this again, for the thousandth time. Then she will cry anyway.

Tomorrow, she will cry not only for the life where she married her teenage sweetheart but for all the other lives too. For the two minutes it takes to wash away the weekend, she will grieve for the Rachels who aren't her: the one who became a doctor and the one who walked on the moon; the one who met her long-ago lover in a hotel and decided not to let him go again; the one who was cruel enough to leave a husband who did nothing but love her.

Tomorrow, Rachel will watch the soap-flecked water swirling round her feet. And when it runs clear, she will shut off the tap, and she will keep watching until it all drains away.

In Retrospect

In the two days he has been away, Tommy's chest has got worse. For a few seconds after Anabelle turns out her bedside lamp, the wheezing and rattling fill the room. He still hasn't made a doctor's appointment. She wants to ask him about it again, but she also doesn't want to ruin this moment of ordinary bedtime calm that is the glue of a million marriages.

She turns on her side to look at him in the gloom. 'How was the exhibition?'

'Fine.'

'Did you sell any drawings?'

'Two.'

'What was the hotel like?'

'Full of retired tourists.'

She hadn't wanted Tommy to go. Not with that cough. They were going up to town for a retrospective of his work at Ruddock's next month, and so Anabelle had wanted him to stay at home this weekend. He had grown thin lately, pale. He needed rest. But Tommy always went. Every exhibition, every major sale, he had to go. Even now, he had to know – had to see for himself – what people thought of his work.

'You're quiet tonight,' Anabelle says when Tommy doesn't offer anything more. 'Are you OK?'

Tommy sighs. His eyes rove the shadows in the ornate plasterwork above their heads. 'I met a friend at the hotel, that's all,' he says. 'A friend from long ago who made me realise how old I am.'

Anabelle laughs and reaches for his hand beneath the covers. She wants to tell him that seventy-three is not so very old, but she feels his cold, thin fingers, and she can't quite form the syllables. She wants to say *I love you*, but the words have lost the zip and zing of youth. It isn't that they have grown old and threadbare; they have not worn out through daily use. It's only that they are middle-aged words – thick-waisted and comfortable; words called over a shoulder as you leave the house; words punctuated by a kiss on the cheek or a backward glance.

So instead, she says, 'Thank you for drawing me.'

It's Tommy's turn to laugh, and his laugh turns into a cough, and he has to sit up. And when he has finished coughing, he looks down at her and smiles. 'Ninety per cent of the people who go to a Tommy Granger exhibition do so to see your face, not my penmanship.'

She loves him for the lie. She loves that he hasn't stopped drawing her as she has grown older. And if sometimes, just sometimes, his preliminary sketches don't look quite like her – if the woman looking out from the paper has sharper features, a wilder look in her eyes – she can forgive that because it's always her in the end. When Tommy leads her into his studio so she can be the first to see the finished picture, it's always her – his wife – who looks back.

'Ruddock Junior wants me to select two portraits of you for the retrospective.' Tommy eases himself down onto his pillow. 'He wants the central piece to be *Grand Jardin* again. But he wants to frame it with two more of you. Which do you think I should choose?'

In the forty-three years they've been married, Tommy has drawn and painted her nineteen times alone and eight times with the girls. Twenty-seven smiling, thinking, reading Anabelles. Anabelle in evening dress or apron, famous squares or private gardens.

'I was wondering about *Mother*,' Tommy says. 'You remember?'

She remembers them all. He had drawn *Mother* when the twins were six weeks old. In it, she is propped up in bed, surrounded by pillows. Lottie is breastfeeding, tucked tight in the crook of her arm. Bessie is asleep, milk-drunk on the embroidered quilt next to her. At the time, Anabelle had resented the hours Tommy was away in his studio, leaving her alone with two babies, each as hungry as the other. But when she saw the picture, she was glad. She was glad that he'd captured the way she is looking at Bessie – something of that early love. When she had three-year-olds who wouldn't sleep, or nine-year-olds who wouldn't do their homework, or teenagers who couldn't believe how unfair she was, she would look at that picture and remember.

'Yes,' she says. 'That one.' She reaches for his hand again. 'And maybe also the last one you did of me.'

The last one. Somehow Anabelle knows that it will be *the* last one, and perhaps that is why she loves it so fiercely, even though she no longer looks young, her tummy sagging as she bends to gather strawberries in the garden.

Tommy runs a thumb over the back of her hand. 'OK. I'll tell Ruddock in the morning.'

They lie in silence, waiting for the sleep that becomes slower to arrive each year.

'This friend,' Anabelle says. 'The one who made you feel old. When did you know each other?'

Tommy shifts to face her. And perhaps he is just a little hesitant. 'When we were teenagers.'

Anabelle imagines Tommy as a teenager. She pictures him with a friend beside him. A girl, perhaps. A young woman with sharper features than she had herself; sharper features and a wilder look in her eyes. A young woman whom he had never drawn, not really. Not like he had drawn her.

'If this friend of yours was here now, would she...' Anabelle hesitates, waits for Tommy to say this friend wasn't a she after all. He stays silent. 'Would she want you to go to a doctor about your cough? Would she be worried, do you think?'

Tommy nods slowly. 'Yes, I suppose she would.'

'I know she's not here.' Anabelle touches a hand to his chest. 'But I am, Tommy. I'm always here.'

'I know.' He takes her hand and presses it to his lips. Then he rolls over to face the opposite wall. 'I'll call them in the morning,' he says. 'I promise.'

Cruising

The moon lights a trail through the ocean, just like the picture in the brochure promised. In its ghost light, Rachel can see the black water stretching away to the edge of the world. Behind her, the sound of strings reaching their crescendo vibrates up the stairwell from the deck below. After dinner, it will be songs from the musicals, or maybe the best of John Williams. Something classy.

She wonders what it would be like to climb over the railing – to step from the deserted deck onto the silver, ripple-less calm. She could walk; she's sure of it. She could walk away from the bright ship lights, and if she walked far enough, there would be nothing but her. She is suddenly hungry for it: for distant horizons in every direction; for whales and dolphins and giant manta rays gliding beneath her feet without looking up; for a moment all alone in the middle of a dark ocean.

He would come looking for her. Francis would cast off the hands that held him, the voices that told him it was too late. He would roll up his chinos and come walking over the water, a phantom in the moonlight. And as he drew near, arms outstretched for rescue, she would feel the ripples of his footsteps; she would feel the soft swell bringing her back to his safety, or, maybe, pulling her beneath the surface.

Curtain Call

When she sees you, her hand goes to her lips. Her eyes widen. For a minute, you think she is going to say your name.

'Come on, Mum.' The man next to her pulls at the cab door. He hasn't seen you. He would think nothing of it if he had. 'Let's get out of the rain.'

For another few seconds, she doesn't move. Then her hand falls away. For an absurd instant, you think she is blowing you a kiss and your fingers twitch in your pocket.

Then she is gone.

'Tommy?' Anabelle is waiting by the door of the taxi behind. 'Are you coming?'

When you've told the cabbie your address, Anabelle turns to you. 'Come on then, you first. What did you think?'

Think. Yes – that's what you need to do. Concentrate on talking to your wife, on not coughing, on not thinking about anybody else.

'It was good,' you say. 'I enjoyed it.'

'I thought it was marvellous.' She sighs. 'Imelda Staunton was perfect, wasn't she?'

Don't look at the cab in front. Don't watch the woman silhouetted in the back. Don't wonder what she is laughing at as she turns to her companion. This is just another evening, like

144

the dozens of others you've spent this way. You know how to do this. When you married Anabelle, you'd never set foot in a theatre, but now you've had decades of practice. You watch the play, and then you talk about performances and pacing and direction – all those things her family taught you from their box in the dress circle in those early years of marriage. You don't talk about a woman who sat three rows away from you, even if she is all you can remember.

Perhaps you should have introduced them. In the interval, over tubs of posh ice cream, you could've brought these two women together: the woman you loved down to your bones before you knew what love was, who took your ring half a century ago and then gave it back, whom you have spent a lifetime trying to forget; and the woman who has loved you, who has kept your ring faithfully on her left hand for four decades, whose face has made your drawings famous. Could you have brought Before and After together like that? Could you all have withstood the collision?

'They're doing *Amadeus* again in January.' Anabelle's voice is studiously casual. 'Did you see? I thought we could go. Bring back memories, wouldn't it?'

You have been embroiled in memories all evening – ever since you saw Her across the foyer – and it takes you a second to retrieve the one Anabelle means. *Amadeus* had been the show you'd seen on the day Anabelle had discovered she was expecting the twins. You'd held hands in the dark auditorium, and every now and then, she would grip you so tightly you knew her thoughts were not up on stage but seven months into the future.

'Simon Callow played Mozart.' Anabelle is looking at you now. 'Before he was famous. Do you remember? It would be nice to go again.'

You know what she needs from you. By offering you *Amadeus*, Anabelle is offering you the chance of another January. Despite the doctors with their headshakes and grave, apologetic diagnoses, despite the drugs that refuse to work, your wife is offering you more time. All she wants – all she needs – is for you to accept it, to accept that this theatre trip might not be the last after all.

The taxi in front scoots through the next junction on amber and disappears down a side road. And maybe, as it turns, you catch a glimpse of a woman inside. Maybe she turns her head to look at you out of the window. Maybe she raises her hands to her lips again – not in shock this time, but in farewell.

Or maybe not.

Anabelle's fingernails are digging into your hand. Her head is turned away. For a minute, you pretend not to see the tears she pretends aren't there. Then you reach across and wipe one from her cheek.

'Simon Callow,' you say. 'And Paul Scofield. I remember it well.'

She smiles. 'We had fun, didn't we?'

You don't know whether she is still talking about one night nearly forty years ago or something more.

'Yes,' you say. 'We did.'

You ride the rest of the way to your London flat in silence, and when you put the key in the door, Anabelle says, 'Penny for your thoughts.'

'I'm thinking how lucky I am to have such a beautiful and intelligent wife.'

She laughs. It's what you always say. She always asks, and you always give the same answer. It has been the private script of your marriage since the very first days. Only this time, you have a fierce, deep need for her to believe you. And you don't know how to say that without making it sound as if every other time you were lying. You weren't lying. You just didn't realise until now how truth changes colour with the light. The last light of day is always the most beautiful, even if it does cast the longest shadows. You wish you knew how to make her understand.

'Bella?' You take her coat from her. 'I was really thinking that you're right. We should go and see *Amadeus* again. Let me know when the tickets are released, and I'll get the best seats in the house, opening night.'

'Really?' She presses her hand to her heart. 'Next year? Do you really want to?'

'Yes.' You place your hand over hers. 'Next year. I really do.'

Passing Acquaintance

Once, it would have been the Births and Marriages Katherine turned to first. Or, if Peter had still been alive, they would've read the headlines, forming Opinions together. Now, as the newspapers circulate the overheated Residents' Lounge, it's the obituaries she turns to. Some days she sees a name she recognises – a famous person she thought was still young or an acquaintance from long ago – and she feels a sadness tinged with victory.

Today it's his name she sees. Top of the column: *Sir Thomas Granger*. And although she has seen a dozen photographs of him over the years, she finds she can only picture him as he was the last time she saw him in person, over fifty years ago. She can still see his nervous smile, the way he removed his hat as she answered the door.

She'd felt sorry for him then. Even as she'd said the words that sent him packing – *Rachel's on honeymoon* – she had pitied him. It wasn't much of a lie. A few weeks later, and it would've been true. What point would there have been in disturbing everything then? It had been for the best. All the same, Katherine had been uneasy. He'd come back. If there was one thing teenage lovers didn't do, it was come back.

Katherine knew what it was like to be in love with a boy whose head was full of dreams – who climbed trees to serenade her through her bedroom window, promising everything: love, adventure, a diamond ring. She also knew what it was like to wait beyond any reasonable hope of Coming Back; to be left with a belly swollen with empty promises; to be a fallen woman before anyone had stopped calling her a girl. She couldn't have allowed the same thing to happen to her daughter.

Katherine reads the obituary again. *Renowned artist. Devoted husband.* If she'd known he was capable of either of those things, it could've been different. She wouldn't have talked Peter into persuading Tommy to leave. She wouldn't have burned Tommy's letters. She wouldn't have typed those replies, making Rachel sound cold enough to make no promises, kind enough to stop him hurrying back to see her. She wouldn't have strung Tommy along until Rachel was safely engaged to Francis, then thrown out his last letters unopened. She hadn't meant to be cruel; it had been necessity, not a game. The odds of Tommy being successful or faithful had been low. To be both had seemed impossible.

It isn't as if Katherine had forced Rachel to marry Francis. She'd wanted to. And they've been happy – Katherine is almost certain of it. When they visit on Sunday afternoons, they seem happy. They talk about Henry and his children or about their twice-yearly cruises. They smile. Sometimes they even hold hands. Doesn't that justify everything?

Francis had been exactly the man Rachel should've been bringing home. A man who was always Francis, never Frank. Katherine hadn't wanted Rachel to marry somebody like her father as girls are supposed to do; she'd wanted her to marry somebody like the man she thought was her father. Somebody like Peter. Good, kind Peter, who couldn't have children of his own and who had swept up Katherine and her sleepless baby and never once breathed a word to suggest he was not Rachel's real dad. He *was* her real dad. He was real in every way except the DNA that gave her brown eyes and a sharp nose and a need to be a little too high, a little too fast, a little more free. Katherine had seen that Francis was like Peter. That was all she needed to see.

If Tommy hadn't come back, Katherine would never have thought of him again. If he hadn't turned up at her door, hat in hand, she wouldn't have found herself going to his exhibitions. She wouldn't have read every article written about him, not bought the coffee table hardback of his best work and kept it under the bed.

It has been a decade since Katherine has made it to one of his exhibitions. The last one was in a tiny Soho gallery just after he'd been offered his knighthood. *Anabelle* it was called – all the drawings he'd done of his wife. Everywhere Katherine turned, Anabelle had been looking down at her. Anabelle, not Rachel. Katherine had wondered what it would've been like to walk those rooms as mother-in-law to the *renowned artist* – to be surrounded by portraits of Rachel, drawn by her *devoted husband*.

It was silly, of course. Rachel and Tommy had been teenagers. It couldn't have lasted. Katherine had only brought them back to earth before they fell. Which is why it was a shock to see Rachel there in Tommy's work, forty years after turning him away. In a corner of the gallery marked *Work in Progress*, the artist had spread some of his sketchbooks. And it was there, from one of the pages, in Anabelle's clothes and with Anabelle's hair, that Rachel had looked out at Katherine. Anyone else might've seen nothing but a sharper, wilder version of the Anabelle that appeared in the gilt frame beside it. But Katherine knew her daughter, and her daughter looked back at her, full of reproach.

The door to the Residents' Lounge opens, and Pat shuffles in. She glances at the paper in Katherine's hand. 'You done with that?'

She takes it from her and eases herself down into the wing-back chair opposite. 'Ooh, the obits – lovely.' She fishes for her glasses. 'Who's it today? Anyone important?'

Katherine turns to look at the wildflower garden beyond the window. 'Don't think so,' she says. 'Nobody we know.'

Everything Since Then

A trail of lights marks Rachel's passage through the house: hallway, kitchen, stairs. Francis follows it to the doorway of the upstairs living room and pauses, waiting for her to notice him.

The living room is Rachel's room. While the rest of the house is furnished with the warm restraint of middle class, the living room is a riot of textures and colours. It is Rachel contained within four walls. Only, today she doesn't fit in. She has lit her oil burner and put on a CD, but she isn't dancing on the chequered rug or lying full-stretch on the sofa conducting an invisible orchestra. In air thick with sandalwood and Gershwin, Rachel appears small and grey. She sits motionless on the edge of the sofa. The newspaper is on her lap.

Francis clears his throat. 'You found it then.'

Rachel startles. 'Oh. It's you,' she says, as if, after fifty years of marriage, he might've been somebody else. She follows the line of his gaze down to the newspaper and frowns. 'This?'

'I thought you'd want to see it.' Francis crosses the room and perches on the sofa beside her. 'The obituary, I mean.'

Rachel runs one finger over the first name. 'Thomas Granger?'

'Yes. Thomas Granger.'

The name tastes strange on Francis's tongue. After so many decades of not saying it, it has a dusty scent, flavoured with the nostalgia of when he first heard it. The name is mini-dresses and Inspector Clouseau, Nina Simone and The Rolling Stones.

It's possible, he supposes, that Thomas Granger is nothing more than nostalgia for Rachel too. She might never speak of him because there is nothing to say. It's possible but unlikely. Francis knows that if there was nothing to say, then Rachel would have said something. If she felt nothing for Tommy Granger, there would've been a dozen times his name passed between them: news of his shows and awards and knighthood. That time last year when they went away for the weekend and found there was an exhibition of his work next to the hotel – she would've said something. But she has been silent and, out of kindness or cowardice, so has he.

Rachel doesn't ask why Francis wanted her to see the obituary. She folds the paper and places it on the coffee table. 'How long have you known?' she says. 'About Tommy.'

'Always.' Francis shrugs. 'I know that you were engaged to him and that you loved him and that your parents made you call it off. I know it wasn't your choice. I knew that before I married you.'

Rachel shakes her head. 'Then you know everything.' Her voice catches. 'You've always known everything.'

Francis has never known everything. He knows that she once loved a man called Tommy Granger, but he has never known whether she still does. He has never quite understood her. Sometimes, he has come close to understanding – he has caught a glimpse – but it has always slid from his peripheral vision. He has learned to be content with that. Somehow they work, him and her, and he daren't peel at the corners of their marriage to find out why in case, beneath the velvet flocking, the plaster begins to crumble.

There are things he should say now, but he has no idea what they are. And so, instead, he turns away. 'I'll leave you in peace.'

When Francis had read the obituary, he'd known he must show it to Rachel. She had to find out here, at home, where she was safe to feel whatever she feels. But he should've waited to read it with her. He should've told her he knew about Tommy years ago and then spent those years taking her to places she would've loved, instead of being too afraid in case they made her regret the life she'd lost – regret marrying him.

And now it's too late.

At the bottom of the stairs, Francis pauses. In his uncertainty about how to comfort his wife over the death of a man she loved, he had forgotten everything important. He remembers now. He remembers that he knows Rachel better than anybody else in the world. He may not understand her, but he knows her. He knows that whoever else she has loved, she loves him. Whatever else she could've chosen, she has continued to choose him. Every day for fifty years, they have woken up and chosen to make footsteps side-by-side in the same dust.

'Francis?'

He turns to see Rachel at the top of the stairs.

'Francis, I'm sorry.'

'What do you have to be sorry for?'

Rachel spreads her hands. 'Everything.'

Francis climbs up a step. 'Do you want to do the Inca Trail?'

'What?'

'Or Mount Kilimanjaro? With a bit of training, we could do Mount Kilimanjaro.' He climbs another two. 'Or the Great Wall of China, if you'd prefer?'

'I don't want to do any of those things.'

'Oh.' He frowns. 'I don't think I can send you to space,' he says. 'I wish I could. I know you want...'

'I don't want to go to space, Francis.'

'You don't?' He walks up to the landing and takes her hand. 'Then what do you want?'

Rachel sinks down to the top step. 'I don't know. I've never really known.'

Francis sits beside her. For a minute, they don't speak. *Rhapsody in Blue* spills out of the living room to fill the air around them. Then he slides an arm around her shoulders.

'How about Brighton?' he says. 'How about a fortnight in Brighton?'

Rachel laughs. And once she starts laughing, she can't stop. And the sound – the sight of her doubled up on the stairs – is so ridiculous and brilliant, that Francis starts laughing too, even though he doesn't quite know what's funny.

When Rachel finally stops, she leans her head on his shoulder. 'Yes,' she says. 'Brighton. I would like that very much.'

★

Perfect Timing

11:54 a.m.

He is early. Francis checks his watch as he jumps off his bicycle. He can't ring the doorbell until exactly midday. Everything has to be perfect. He wheels his bike down the narrow passageway that runs down the side of Rachel's house and props it against the wall. He straightens his jacket and pulls the bunch of carnations from where they stick out of the saddlebag, plucking off a crushed petal.

He peers round the corner to the front of Rachel's house. Nobody in sight. He slips past her dad's Cortina and into the covered porch, checks his watch again and takes a deep steadying breath. Five more minutes, and he can ring the bell.

11:56 a.m.

'Are you going to get changed?'

The voice comes so close to him, Francis takes a step back. Then he realises that it is coming from inside the house, through the open sitting-room window on the other side of the porch.

'He said he'd be here at twelve, and you're still in those awful jeans.' He recognises Katherine's voice. *My future mother-*

in-law, he thinks to himself. It sounds good. 'Go and put a dress on.'

When Rachel answers her mother, she is too far from the window for Francis to make out the words, but he knows that tone. His Rachel. Can he call her his? They've been going steady for four months now – is that enough? He touches the box in his inside pocket for luck.

'You like Francis, don't you?' Katherine's voice is sharp.

Another murmur.

'Well, there you are then. What's the problem?'

Problem? No, there can't be a problem. This day – this moment – has to be just right. No problems.

'For goodness' sake, Rachel. Please tell me this isn't about Tommy Granger still?'

There certainly can't be a problem called Tommy Granger. Not now. They've done it all perfectly so far: meeting at a respectable disco, going to see *The Graduate* at the pictures, holding hands on the way home, meeting the parents. They've done everything how it ought to be done – exactly how Katherine and Peter might expect. Nobody has said anything about a Tommy Granger.

'Sweetheart.' Katherine's voice is softer now. 'Tommy's been gone for over a year and a half. If he was serious, don't you think he would've come back? You broke the engagement and...'

'You made me.' Francis does hear Rachel this time.

'We didn't make you. We only asked you to wait a bit. And we were right, weren't we? I'm sorry, darling, but if Tommy was that serious about marrying and whisking you off to live in Paris, he would have written, wouldn't he? He was a third-rate artist, Rachel, not first-rate husband material. Don't you throw away your chance with a nice man like Francis over

158

some teenage fantasy. You don't want to be a shorthand typist forever, do you?'

There is a long pause. Francis feels the ring box in his pocket weighing him down, rooting him to the herringbone tiles.

'You're happy with Francis, aren't you?'

Francis strains for Rachel's answer. Only a murmur.

Katherine tuts. 'Then what more do you want? Because let me tell you, the life Francis could give you would look pretty rosy from a filthy French boarding house with a baby and nothing to eat.' Her voice grows louder as she nears the window. 'If you feel anything at all for this man, then pop upstairs and change into something pretty, hmmm?'

11:59 a.m.

He shouldn't have come early. What a stupid thing to do – to come early and loiter in the porch like this, as if the minute and hour could make any difference to who he is and who Rachel is and who they could be.

12:01 p.m.

He could leave. He could walk away now and say nothing, like this man – this Tommy Granger – did. He could throw the flowers in the nearest bin and try to forget.

12:02 p.m.

Or he could stay. He could keep the box in his pocket – pretend it was just another Sunday lunch. He could give the flowers to Katherine and say he bought them on a whim for the mother of his girlfriend. Then he could withdraw honourably – leave it a little longer between phone calls, be too busy to see Rachel a few more nights in the week.

12:03 p.m.

Or he could give the flowers to Rachel after all. He could offer the flowers and his ring and let her choose for herself what happens after now.

12:04 p.m.

The one thing he will not do is make it hard for her. He won't mention the name that hurts her, whatever else he does.

12:05 p.m.

Leave and say nothing.

12:06 p.m.

Stay and say nothing. Give the flowers to Katherine.

12:07 p.m.

Stay and say nothing and spend the rest of his life saying everything except that one nothing. Give the flowers to the woman he loves.

Francis thinks of the way Rachel laughs politely when they listen to *Round the Horne* with her parents after dinner, and the way she grins at him as she retunes the wireless to Radio Caroline as soon as they are out of the room. His Rachel. His Rachel who loved a man called Tommy Granger. Who maybe still does.

12:11 p.m.

The door opens, and Francis jumps.

'There you are.' Katherine beams at him. 'I was just popping next door to borrow some apple sauce for lunch.' She stands back. 'Make yourself at home.'

And Francis finds himself on the doormat, in the hall, at the foot of the stairs. And Rachel is walking down them towards him in the green dress she was wearing at the disco that time. And everything after now is rushing towards him at a speed he isn't ready for – dazzling him with maybes and if onlys.

Rachel stops on the bottom step and leans forward to smell the carnations. 'Beautiful,' she says, and her eyes meet his. 'Are they for me?'

Last Respects

At the lychgate, Anabelle pauses. The February sun has barely cleared the horizon, leaving curls and rivers of mist in the valley beyond the church, and yet she is not the first one here. For a moment, she stands beneath the dripping yew, watching the dark figure beside the grave.

It is a woman. Even from the other side of the churchyard, Anabelle can see that. The bunch of daffodils the woman holds at her side are the only splash of colour against her sombre dress. Her head is bowed under a black hat. As Anabelle watches, the woman stoops and places the flowers on Tommy's grave. Anabelle shifts her own posy of daffodils to the other hand, quietly lifts the latch on the gate.

'Mrs Granger?'

The voice comes from behind Anabelle. She turns to face a tall man in a dark overcoat, hat respectfully in his hand.

'It is Mrs Granger, isn't it?' He smiles. 'I recognise you from the portraits. I'm Francis. I didn't know your husband, but he was a great artist. I'm sorry for your loss.'

It is two weeks since Anabelle was last here. Two weeks since she stood in the church porch with Lottie and Bessie beside her, offering her hand to the line of mourners following Tommy's coffin to the grave.

I'm so sorry, Charlotte.

So sorry, Anabelle.

We're so sorry, Elizabeth.

So sorry for your loss.

It had seemed a formality then. It was what you said at funerals. This man, though, seemed different. Anabelle believed him.

'Thank you.'

'My wife knew him a long time ago,' Francis says. He nods towards the woman by the grave. 'She didn't want to disturb the private funeral but did want to pay her respects. He meant a lot to her.'

And Anabelle knows then. She knows who this woman is. She is the Woman Who Is Not Anabelle. Tommy had drawn Anabelle so many times – enough to make her face famous – but his pictures had always started out with someone else. With Her. Each portrait would start with a wild, instinctive sketch; Tommy would have to find the root and rhythm of his art before he could get down to the details of Anabelle's clothes and face. And the root and rhythm of his art was this woman.

'It's her,' Anabelle says.

It must seem a strange comment to the man beside her, but when she turns to offer some explanation, she finds he is nodding already.

'Yes,' he says. 'It's her.'

She swallows and looks down at the gravel. 'Tommy never talked about your wife,' she says. 'Did they...? Were they...?'

'As teenagers.' Francis nods. 'They were something as teenagers, I believe. Not since.'

Anabelle turns her gaze back across the graveyard. 'They never forgot.' She shuts her eyes. 'They couldn't forget.'

Francis lays a hand on her arm. 'They never went back, though, did they? They never searched for each other.'

Anabelle looks up into his kind, lined face. She doesn't know him. She doesn't have conversations like this with men she doesn't know. She doesn't have them with anybody.

'Why didn't they?' she says. 'Why didn't they go back?'

'I don't know.' Francis shrugs. 'Maybe they didn't really want to. Maybe they had enough. They had...' He tails off, shrugs again.

'Us,' Anabelle says. 'Yes. Maybe.'

She slips quietly through the lychgate and across the grass, leaving dark tracks through the dew. When she is only a few steps away, the woman looks up. She sees Anabelle's face, and her eyes widen. She takes a step away.

'Sorry, I was just...'

Anabelle holds out a hand to stop her. She crouches to add her own daffodils to the mound of earth still piled high over the grave. Then she walks to the woman's side.

'I'm sorry,' the woman says again. 'I'm sorry for your loss.'

Anabelle thinks of her loss: the space on the other side of the bed and the sentences she has to finish for herself. Then she thinks of everything before her loss. She thinks of Lottie and Bessie and all the portraits in the world where her face and Tommy's name lie indelibly, eternally together.

She slides her hand into the crook of the woman's arm. 'Thank you,' she says. 'I'm sorry for your loss too.'

For a minute, they stand arm-in-arm. Then the woman eases herself free and walks back to her husband. And Anabelle is left alone beside a grave lit with late winter sunlight and the two bunches of daffodils side-by-side upon it.

Feet on the Ground

The oak is different now. Its branches stretch away from them as they climb, twisting and creaking. A few minutes ago, as they walked across the frost-sharp grass, it had been a skeletal giant, stark against the heavy sky. Now they are in its arms, it has become a nebulous, untouched thing. It has a beginning but no end, roots but no tips. She doesn't know what they will find at the top, or even if there is a top anymore. But she keeps climbing.

There is a ball of mistletoe above her, vivid against the grey. As she reaches out to pluck a berry, she sees her hands. Her hands are different too. The liver spots are gone. Her skin is tightening, veins no longer pressing to escape. When she looks down, the man who stood at the foot of the tree with her is gone, replaced by an earlier version. His white hair is grey, seeping into black as she watches him haul himself up behind her. His shoulders broaden, his cheeks fill out. When he catches sight of her face, he smiles as if she's a friend she hasn't seen for years.

She begins to climb again. Branches bud and curl out of the trunk to meet her. With each step, she gains strength, joints loosen, lungs expand. Months and years stream from her back into the winter dusk. She is being unmade. The rough edges of age and disappointment are growing smooth. The pits and scars of seventy-eight years are melting away. And now she knows that when they reach the top, they will be formless again. That is what waits for them. Newness. The chance to try again – to unchoose all her wrong choices.

She'll do it better this time. She'll keep all her New Year's resolutions. She'll follow her heart and her dreams and her doctor's advice.

'Look.'

She stops at the sound of his voice.

'You can see our house from up here.'

He is pointing out across the fields to the house that isn't theirs anymore. It hasn't belonged to them for thirty years. The windows are lit, there is a wreath on the door. And she remembers why they came. To see this. To visit the tree she climbed with their son. To remember.

'We used to watch for your car,' she says. 'On summer evenings.' She steps down to a branch beside him. 'And when we saw it, we would race each other home across the field.'

He smiles, and the crow's feet at his eyes deepen. She feels her back stiffen. With each second, they remain, time settles back on their shoulders, diffuses into their blood.

'I used to see you coming,' he says. 'And I never knew which one I wanted to get to me first. I was so desperate to see both of you.'

She hadn't known that. She'd assumed he was humouring them as he waited on the doorstep. He would rather have been three minutes quicker to the sofa and his whisky. She had judged him for that – for those thoughts she'd thought he had.

If they keep climbing, all that will be gone. Every mis-understanding – every time they said something they didn't mean or didn't say something they should have – will be erased. Every mistake. Every frustration.

The molar she had filled fifteen years ago begins to ache again. The ankle she twisted last year, walking in the foothills of the Alps with her granddaughter, throbs in the cold. She grasps at the next branch, pulling herself higher. Next time, she will eat more fibre. She'll drink two litres of water a day, a small glass of red wine twice a week. She will visit her mother more often.

For a few minutes, they climb, she then he.

Next time, she'll never forget a birthday and always wear jeans that fit her properly. She will marry in a whirlwind of passion. She'll not settle for contentment; she will aim at ecstasy.

She tilts her head back as far as she dares. Maybe she can see the top now. Maybe they're close. She reaches for the next handhold.

'Do you remember the Christmas we got a tree so big we couldn't get it in the house?' His voice seems further away. 'We had to decorate it in the garden.'

She looks down. He has stopped climbing. He's sitting on a branch, looking up at her. 'Do you remember?'

She nods.

'And do you remember the time we went to Clacton and Henry caught all those crabs using our sandwiches as bait?'

'We had to go and get chips for lunch,' she says. 'And we couldn't be cross at him because he was so pleased with himself.'

She eases herself down onto her branch and sits with her back against the trunk.

'Do you remember the nights we took turns pacing the landing with a crying baby?'

She smiles. 'Nine paces in each direction.'

'Do you remember all the Saturdays we did nothing much because it rained?' He is still watching her. 'Do you remember all the times we made the perfect cup of tea or found there were two biscuits left in the tin after all?'

'No.' She shakes her head. 'Not really.'

'No,' he says. 'Me neither.'

Above them, the tree groans and creaks. She looks up into the web of branches. Everything that is gone will be gone.

The flesh on her hands is failing – the skin growing loose around it. Everything they remember, everything they don't – they can leave it behind. They can be new.

For another moment they sit, looking out at a house that doesn't belong to them anymore.

'It's getting dark,' he says.

'Yes.' She sighs. 'It is.' She reaches out a leg to find a firm foothold. 'We'd best get down. Before we fall.'

ACKNOWLEDGEMENTS

My first heartfelt thank-you is to David Borrowdale and Reflex Press for publishing this novella. I am also deeply indebted to the editor Michael Loveday, without whom this book would never have got off the ground (I know that's a cliché, Michael, but please note my correct use of the word 'whom').

Thank you both to my parents and to the hive mind of social media, whose generous answers to my many questions allowed my characters to do things accurately – from gambling in the 1950s to getting drunk in the 1990s (via 1960s school tights and the layout of Heathrow thirty years ago). Any errors are entirely my own. Thanks also to those who read earlier versions of these stories and cheered me on.

I am forever grateful to God for all my blessings, most especially for my husband and biggest cheerleader Paul. (You know that you and me, we could do anything.)

Finally, thank you to all the inspiring female pioneers of space flight – those written about in this book and those I couldn't squeeze in: Helen Sharman, Mae Jemison, Wally Funk and so many other brave and fabulous women. You rock.

~

The author and publisher wish to thank the editors of the publications in which the following stories first appeared, online or in print:

'Everything After Now' first appeared in *Flash 500*, December 2016; 'Dead Cert' – as 'Odds-On', *Flash 500*, February 2020; 'Wildflowers: A History' – as 'Wildflower', *InterAct Stroke Support*, December 2017.

REFLEX PRESS

Reflex Press is an independent publisher based in Abingdon, Oxfordshire, committed to publishing bold and innovative books by emerging authors from across the UK and beyond.

Since our inception in 2018, we have published award-winning short story collections, flash fiction anthologies, and novella-length fiction.

www.reflex.press
@reflexfiction